THE PITCH

BUSINESS LESSONS LEARNED ON THE SOCCER FIELD

LINDA J. LORD

iUNIVERSE, INC.
NEW YORK   BLOOMINGTON

The Pitch
Business Lessons Learned on the Soccer Field

iUniverse books may be ordered through booksellers or by contacting:

*iUniverse
1663 Liberty Drive
Bloomington, IN 47403
www.iuniverse.com
1-800-Authors (1-800-288-4677)*

*Because of the dynamic nature of the Internet, any Web addresses or
links contained in this book may have changed since publication and may
no longer be valid.*

*ISBN: 978-1-4401-7453-7 (sc)
ISBN: 978-1-4401-7454-4 (ebk)*

Printed in the United States of America

iUniverse rev. date: 10/13/2009

Also by Linda J. Lord

31 Days Toward Maximum Living

To:

My son, Nolan Tipping and his love of soccer

My daughter, Livia

My husband, Raymond

*John Lepera, who served as inspiration and Nolan's 2007
house league soccer coach.*

*And most importantly to the Lord of my life who bestows
all gifts and talents.*

Linda

1

I rolled out of bed in much the same mood I had rolled into it only a few hours before – miserable which was a shame because I usually felt pretty good in the mornings. I was as they say, a morning person. I always had been. My most productive time of day was usually between 5 and 7 am. But don't expect much out of me after 9 at night. It made me a lousy date, actually.

The sun streamed through the slats of my shutters. I had opted for them instead of curtains. I wasn't a big fan of blocking things out. At least not the pleasant things. If only those same shutters could block out the reality of my business. Now that I would have gladly accepted.

My cash flow was a disaster, my marketing plan was ineffective, my employees were whiney, and I realized that I had absolutely no idea how to run a business. It had seemed like the answer to a prayer when I found myself out of work and in possession of this great business plan I had put together a few years before my son was born. Of course, I had been married and any business I might have started back then would have been more of a glorified hobby to keep me from going insane at home. Not the best recipe for a new business venture, but stuck in bad economic times and wanting to prove to myself that I could make a living in the highly competitive event-planning industry, I set forth. I was organized. I had a background in planning. I had handled all types of people. What else was there? Funny, but no one tells you – or I didn't listen – to how much more there is!

It was the middle of May and I knew that my half year actuals were going to fall far short of my projections. I wasn't exactly sure what the problem was, or perhaps more accurately, what the problems – plural – were, but I knew that it wasn't looking good. I had all the right support around me: an accountant, a banker, a bookkeeper, administrative staff, a marketing specialist, and a business advisor. How could I have all the right tools and still be in the mess I found myself? The answer to that question would have to wait, because my "job before my job" awaited me.

"Justin," I called before entering the bathroom, "Time to get up for school."

My fourteen year old son grumbled about having to get out of bed, but used to his morning protests I proceeded on schedule with my routine. He was definitely not a morning person. As I made the coffee and put bread in the toaster, I wondered how many other single mother business owners there were out there, making breakfast and dreading the start of another day; unsure and insecure, but too proud to admit it.

"Mornin' Mom," Justin said, planting a kiss on my cheek.

"Hey, honey. How'd you sleep?"

"Pretty good." Then seeing his breakfast, his tone became much less pleasant. " Not toast again! Mom, I'm trying to eat healthy. You got my stuff ready?"

"Stuff?" I replied blankly.

"Soccer practice. Tonight."

"Oh, that. Sure."

"You forgot, didn't you?"

"Not exactly," I hedged.

"Don't lie to me, Mom. I've been waiting my whole life to make this regional team. "

He could be so melodramatic. I had no idea where he got that.

"I can't believe you forgot," he continued.

I decided to ignore the bait. "What do you need for tonight?"

"The usual: shorts, socks, shin pads, shirt, cleats."

"Don't your old cleats still fit?" I was secretly hoping they did because I wasn't sure where the money was going to come from to buy new ones.

"No."

"Are you sure?"

"I'm sure."

I closed my eyes and rubbed my forehead in frustration. Justin knew what that meant.

"We don't have the money for my shoes, do we?"

"I'll find the money."

"Where? You're always telling me how we don't have any."

"You let me figure that out, okay?" The toast popped. "Let's have some breakfast."

"I don't want any breakfast. I'll grab an apple and eat it on the way."

"So, it's not breakfast you don't want, it's THIS breakfast."

I turned to get my plate from the cupboard. I took a moment to admire what a great job the coat of white paint had done in hiding some of the dings on the old doors. As I did, I heard Justin. I'm not sure whether he was mumbling under his breath to himself or if he was intending me to hear, but I heard nonetheless.

"I can't stand being poor. I wish she'd just admit she can't run a business and get a real job."

He grabbed his backpack and an apple and left without saying goodbye.

Ungrateful brat, I muttered to myself. That wasn't exactly the truth, though. We had been on our own for 10 years and he wasn't the type of kid that usually made my life difficult with unrealistic demands or disrespectful behavior. I should have remembered about soccer. It was the only thing he had ever asked of me. It was the only sport he had ever played. And it had given him something to focus on when his dad walked out.

But still, his words stayed with me all day. I wasn't sure if he had meant them to hurt me, but they had. I was already feeling like a failure. Maybe he had a point. Did I deserve to stay in business? What 'real job' was I even qualified for?

I wasn't in the best of moods when I finally did get to the office. I walked through the stream of staff questions and closed the door a little too abruptly behind me. My desk was a disaster. There were papers everywhere and unanswered phone messages in a sloppy stack next to the handset. Yesterday's half-full cup of cold coffee stared up at me. That was what I needed – another coffee. I walked back through the offices, ignoring everyone and breathed deeply as I left the building. What a relief that long morning was over! All seven minutes of it! When I forced myself to return I just went through the motions. People came at me with questions I couldn't answer. I made phone calls that I couldn't remember. I shouldn't have let Justin's off-handed comment so completely influence my day, but that just goes to show where my head was.

I stopped by the sports store on the way home and put Justin's cleats on my credit card. Fortunately, he and I had been in the store a few weeks back and he had selected the style and size he needed, so there wasn't much challenge in choosing the cleats. The real challenge was in paying for them. I held my breath as the salesperson processed the purchase. I was half expecting the machine to read my card and laugh, but it didn't, and the transaction was approved. I had grown accustomed to the sinking feeling that accompanies the space between processing and approval. Justin was right about being cash poor. I hated it too.

I left the box on top of Justin's soccer bag. I'm not sure what I was expecting when he saw it, but I was glad that the boy who came to thank me was the Justin I knew and not the one who had been in my kitchen that morning.

"Can we afford these?" he asked.

"I got a little wiggle room."

"Seriously, Mom. I don't expect you to get these for me if we can't afford it. I can pay for them."

"How?"

"I could get a job or something." He paused for effect, "You hiring?"

I laughed as I always did when Justin got the better of me. He had a way of making me smile when I had no intention of it.

"Not today, but I'll keep you in mind when I franchise."

"How much?" he asked, turning each cleat over carefully in his hands. "They're the nice ones, Mom. Thanks."

"You don't want to know and you're welcome. Just play well."

"You got it."

2

WHEN THERE'S THREATENING WEATHER, DRESS ACCORDINGLY

I had been taking Justin to soccer practices and games since he was four years old. I still couldn't get used to sitting on an open field, wrapped in a thick blanket, and shivering for hours, all in the name of sport. I decided to hang out on the sidelines to offer my support for his first practice. The truth was, it was a much needed distraction. I couldn't say the day had been a complete disaster; a few prospects had called in. I was hanging on but it wasn't where I needed it to be. I wrapped the blanket more tightly around myself, feeling the bite of the wind on my face. I watched the boys scurrying around the field, going through their drills. I could hear them complaining amongst themselves about the weather and how the coach must hate them already to make them endure such conditions; and then I heard something interesting.

"Come on over here for a minute, boys," the coach called, swinging his arms in that 'get over here, now' way that we do. "I just want to remind you that it's May. May weather is still unpredictable. You might be out here in scorching heat, biting winds, or a torrential downpour. It won't matter. If there isn't lightning, you'll be on the pitch, so look up. If the weather is threatening, dress accordingly. The practice will happen."

Interesting, I thought to myself. I sat shivering in the cold. Shivering from the weather, but also from the realization that what he said had some validity in business, too. I had seen my share of 'threatening weather', but had I dressed accordingly? Had I dressed my business and myself to stay warm and dry? If I was inadequately prepared, how could I expect my business to do any better?

The truth was that I hadn't been prepared for much in my life. I had just kind of let it happen. That could explain a lot. I had been seventeen when I met Justin's dad. He had been such a charmer. Tall, lean, social; things I admired, but wasn't. I wasn't fat or short, just kind of average. At 5'4" I was never the tallest person in my circle of friends. Circle might actually be an exaggeration. I'm not sure it was even a semi-circle. I was thrilled when Jim asked me out. I wasn't sure why he did, but it was exciting. Maybe he saw something in me…you know how a teenage girl thinks. I should have known from that first date that things weren't right. He was late picking me up and explained that he had had to take his study partner home. His study partner, right. It didn't take me long to realize that he was studying her anatomy, but I kept telling myself how lucky I was to have a guy like him interested in me. A girl can make a lot of stuff up to keep from facing reality.

I was concerned that I was doing that again, with the business. That I was making it all seem better than it actually was. Maybe it was time to wake up and listen to what might be sound advice. I hadn't been much of a counsel seeker in the past and look where I ended up. It might be time to try to see if there was something that could be learned, no matter the source.

I hoped that the coach would say more things that I might be able to apply to my flailing business. He did offer some other tidbits, but it was the concept of preparation that I continued to consider. I had to admit that I hadn't done very much to ensure the business was ready for what we were currently facing. I also realized that the first real work that had to be done was staring at me in the mirror. I had to rethink my business and who I wanted to be as a business owner. The days of playing at it were in one sense over, and in another way just beginning. I was going to take the time during each of Justin's practices to really listen to what the coach was saying and to consider how it might apply to me and my business. Armed with this fresh perspective, and dare I say it, enthusiasm about tomorrow, I met my son at the edge of the field. I asked him how he thought things went.

"What's wrong with you?" he asked.

"Nothing."

"You seem weird."

He was right. It did feel weird to be looking forward to getting up in the morning and heading into the office.

I laid in bed that night mulling over what I would do and how I could better prepare my business, and myself for all kinds of weather. In a maternal moment, I also realized that I had not been properly preparing Justin for life, either. I was constantly complaining about our circumstances without showing him that I was actively trying to change anything. I needed to be a better role model for him. I needed to give him opportunities to develop the skills for life. I eventually drifted off to sleep, excited about what I was about to begin.

I leapt out of bed even before the alarm the next morning. I tapped on Justin's door and didn't wait for the growl. No one was going to dampen my spirits today. I was ready to dress for the weather.

What I didn't yet realize was the hurricane that awaited me when I sat down at my desk. There was a message from the bank. That was never a good sign. I delayed calling for as long as the churning in my stomach would allow, but I couldn't hide forever. I'm not proud to admit that the branch manager placed a second call before I returned the first one.

"Good morning," he said abruptly. "I phoned you yesterday."

"Yes," I answered meekly, "I'm just getting to my messages." I hated lieing but I determined it was still better than admitting I was a coward.

"There seems to be a problem with your account."

"A problem?"

"You are overdrawn on your business account and if you recall, you agreed that we could take money from your personal account to cover any overdrafts. " I waited for the bomb. "But there isn't any money there, either. You need to make a deposit today or I will have to start returning cheques as NSF."

"Please don't do that," I begged. "I have a couple of clients coming in to pay in the next few days. Could you give me until the end of the week?"

"Two days. That's the best I can do."

We must have finished the conversation with pleasantries, but frankly I have no idea what they might have been. How was I going to come up with the money in two days?

At dinner that night, Justin was struggling to say something. I assumed it had to do with soccer, but he could tell I was distracted.

"What's up, Mom?"

"The bank called today. I'm overdrawn."

"Oh." Justin looked at his plate as though the answer to world peace was hidden somewhere between the noodles and the hamburg. My hunch was probably right; he wanted to ask me for something.

"What are you looking for?" I asked.

"What?"

"In your food."

"Nothin."

"I hate to ask, Justin, but you might have to get a part time job to help out."

"Or you could get a REAL job!"

I was stunned by the intensity of his response.

"Justin."

"No, seriously. I want a normal life where we have enough money for groceries, and cleats, and soccer camp."

"Is that what this is about? Your soccer camp. You haven't heard anything I've said."

"You haven't said anything I haven't heard a thousand times. Your business sucks and you refuse to admit it. You want me to get a job, fine, I'll get a job, but the money goes to me and my soccer." Justin slid his chair back, slamming it into the kitchen wall and stormed out of the house. When the weather becomes threatening, dress appropriately. I had better grab a rain coat and boots; this storm didn't look like it was going to pass very quickly.

3

The Coach Knows the Game

Later that week, I again found myself sitting on the sidelines of Justin's practice. I certainly wasn't in the elated mood I had been when we left last time. My relationship with Justin was still strained, but he had taken a part time job at a local coffee shop. I had reluctantly agreed that his pay could be used for soccer. It wasn't that that hadn't been my intention all along, I just didn't want to reward his outburst at the table. He was changing. I knew that would happen once he became a teenager, but I really missed that sweet boy that I had first brought to the soccer field many years before.

I settled in to listen as the coach started practice.

"Glad to see you came back, boys. Nice to see you have your warm-up jackets on this afternoon. By this point in your soccer 'careers' I shouldn't have to tell you the rules of the game, but I should probably remind you that I am a player. I still play. I love the game. So, there will be times that I will be out on the field with you. I love to scrimmage. I'll be out there mixing it up with you. But there will be other times when I have to watch from the side. And even during those times when I'm with you, remember that I am not one of you. You will never be my equal. I know the game and I know how I want it played. If you challenge me, I'll toss you. Clear?" The boys nodded; either in fear or acceptance. I doubt the coach cared which it was. He just wanted compliance.

As I sat and watched the practice unfold, I began to believe that the coach did know his game. He anticipated where the boys would go. He understood how each play was to be executed. He could predict where a shot would land. At one point, he called the boys over to form a huddle and reviewed some basic rules of engagement.

"For some of you, this will be your first year in this type of league. There are different rules here. The games are more physical. The players are more aggressive. You will have to improve your game, or you will find yourself on the bench – a lot."

I questioned his tactics. I thought he was a little harsh for a man dealing with fourteen year old boys. Or maybe he knew something I didn't. Coddling Justin certainly hadn't been the answer for me. He liked to be challenged. He needed a male role model who was going to push him. I could see that. It seemed to be the right combination of the love of the game and expectations of high performance.

Since it would seem I was learning as much about myself and my business at these practices as I was about soccer, I wondered to myself how I might apply the coach's words to my current situation.

The first question was obvious. Did I know the game I was playing? And the obvious answer was yes. I was in the event planning business. But as I spent more time considering my answer, I became less certain. Had I really done all that was necessary to understand the game and the rules of engagement? I did have a business plan, but it was hopelessly out of date. I had used old numbers to justify a new business. Things had changed in the past fourteen years. Did I know what and by how much? I wasn't really sure how my business plan reflected meeting the needs of my target market. Once again, I had been in such a rush to do something that I had impulsively jumped at the first thing that looked like it would solve my problems.

I know that people start businesses for a variety of reasons, but mine was so lame. I was unemployed and I was afraid I wasn't going to find work before the bank took my house. I wasn't the type of person who had accumulated great reserves. I was a single mom, eking out an existence in a job that paid just a few dollars a week more than I required to live. As I look back, what self respecting bank manager would lend someone like me enough money to open a business? He must have been laughing all the way to the vault.

I didn't know the first thing about my business game. I had to try to become the coach of my business, but where to start? I supposed it was possible to regroup and start doing the research that I should have done in the first place. It wasn't too late to learn about my industry.

I walked up to the coach at the end of practice. I'm quite sure my son was having an anxiety attack when he saw me striding confidently toward them. I wasn't exactly sure what I was doing. It might have proven to be an embarrassing moment, but I wanted to do something and this seemed like the most expedient choice.

"Mom? What are you doing?"

"I want to talk to your coach for a minute."

"Why?"

"Don't worry," I assured him, "I won't embarrass you."

I could tell by the look he shot me that he was not convinced.

"Excuse, me," I stated politely, "May I have a word with you?"

Not looking up from his clipboard, the coach answered. "Whose mother are you?"

"Justin Robertson."

Again without looking up, "Good kid. He'll get lots of play time."

"Well, thank you, but that's not why I want to speak to you."

That, for some reason, got his attention. "Then what?"

"I've been listening to you coach the boys and I've been learning a lot myself."

He, like most men whose egos you stroke, was now listening. "Really?"

"Yes, really. I have been taking what you're teaching them and applying it to my business."

"And what business is that?"

"I operate an event-planning business."

"What does that mean?"

"I work with individuals who want a professional to plan their event."

"That's a business?"

"Yes."

"How did you get into it?"

"A series of unfortunate events?" I joked, but he didn't even crack a smile.

"So what have you learned?"

"That I don't know very much about running a business."

"That's a problem."

"I'd say. And now I find myself in a severe cashflow shortfall."

"You sound surprised."

"I didn't realize things had gone so far. I counted on my staff to monitor the KPI."

Looking at his watch, I could tell he hoped I soon got to the point.

"So I was wondering if you'd mind coaching me, too?"

"I'm not in your business. I don't know how I could be of any help."

"I don't want you to help me with the business. I just want to be able to hear what you're telling the boys, so I can apply what's relevant. And there are some things I can't hear from where I sit on the far side of the field."

"What are you asking, exactly?"

"Can I sit close to where you are, so I can hear everything?

"How does Justin feel about that?"

I looked around and realized he had long since headed to the car. "Guess I better check."

"If it's okay with him, then I'm fine with it."

"Thanks."

He waved at me as he walked away. I felt a little uneasy about telling Justin what I had done, but I hoped he'd understand.

"NO WAY!" He screamed. "Do you have to ruin everything?"

It was a quiet ride home and a silent morning following my announcement that Justin's coach was allowing me to eavesdrop on his work with the boys. I suppose I didn't fully appreciate the spot I was putting my son in, but I justified it by telling myself that when the business was more viable, he would be grateful for whatever steps I took to provide for us.

"Are you going to talk to me this morning?"

Nothing.

"Justin, I don't want you to be upset with me."

He glared at me. "You're a joke. You can't make it on your own, so you think spying on me is going to help?"

"I'm not spying on you. I just think the coach tells you things that could help me run my business. That's all."

"Do you think he's cute, Mom?"

"What?"

"He's married, so don't get any ideas."

"Trust me, Justin, I have enough to deal with without getting involved with a guy right now."

"Whatever."

He turned to leave the kitchen.

"Justin. I'm not finished talking to you about this."

"Well, I'm finished listening." He grabbed his backpack and slammed the door on his way out, leaving me alone with the silence that followed.

I got to the office just before 8:30. I spent a few minutes surfing on the internet, looking for locations to host a wellness conference and trying to find a variety of business models that might help me understand my game. I realized that I was still very committed to the idea of my business. I liked the fact that I could help people put together an event that raised money for a charity, celebrated a significant occasion, or rewarded outstanding employees. What I did still mattered to me. I guessed that was a good place to start. I looked around and decided I needed to rethink my environment. If I was to enter the space for the first time, would I feel welcome? Would I be able to know, just by walking through the front door, that my event was in professional hands?

I decided to spend every moment that wasn't scheduled with clients to focus on examining my business with fresh eyes. It might be difficult to assess it objectively, but I knew that if I ran into trouble I had a team of people that would help me.

I started with a big piece of paper. I wrote down everything it took to run my business: inventory, promotion, marketing, sales, bookkeeping, accounting, client management, reception, scheduling, follow-up, delivery of service, research, and business planning. Then, I honestly asked myself who was doing each of those things. The truth was that many of the elements to run a strong business were either left to chance, someone else, or completely undone. It was a sobering realization that under those conditions I couldn't expect my business to flourish – it was starving to death. Here I was, a professional at booking locations, entertainment, and food so everyone went away feeling great, and my own business was not great at all.

4

COACHES ASSESS PERFORMANCE AND RECOGNIZE POTENTIAL

Justin was still on his silent protest when I picked him up after school. I dropped him off at the Coffee House where he was working part time as a bus boy.

"I think I'll come in and grab a coffee."

"How about take out?" Justin asked. "Or are you going to bug my boss for business advice, too?"

"You know what, Justin, I have just about had it with your attitude."

He shrugged and walked away.

I wasn't doing very well as a mother these days. I was so distracted that I couldn't give Justin my full attention. I was sure he was going through something, but I couldn't put my finger on it. It felt like everything was just beyond my reach — and influence. I skipped the coffee.

I fixed a nice supper that night. I had taken the time to plan the meal and make it more nutritious than usual. I hoped that Justin would appreciate the effort and see that his having to take the job wasn't just me being evil.

The meal was a moderate success.

"Hows' the job?" I asked.

"Pretty good."

"What do you do?"

"I bus tables, Mom. I pick up what other people leave behind." He paused. "Kind of like my life."

I was crushed. He had no way of knowing the death blow he had just delivered. I could feel the heat in my cheeks and the stinging in my eyes. I excused myself and fled to the isolation of my bedroom. I wept openly as I lay across my bed.

I heard a gentle knock.

"Mom? Are you okay? I'm really sorry. I shouldn't have said that."

No, he shouldn't have; but he did.

"Mom?"

I remained silent. I heard him walk away a few minutes later. My pity party was short lived, though, as I had to drive him to soccer practice. Justin tried to engage me in conversation but I was uncooperative. He could live in my world for a while.

As we pulled into the parking lot, he looked over at me.

"Where are you sitting?"

"I would like to sit so I can hear the coach."

"You won't ask him anything in front of the team?"

"I won't embarrass you, Justin."

"Cool."

Justin grabbed his bag from the trunk. I saw a couple of his friends walking across the field.

"Why don't you catch up with Mark and Tony? I'll be along in a few minutes."

He nodded the way teens do when they have to acknowledge a parent, but don't want to be caught by their friends doing it. I watched him walk away. It was more of a swagger actually. He had gotten so tall. His short sandy brown hair was gelled a little in the front as boys were wearing it now. He had a style about him and he did his best to fit it on a limited budget. I knew it wasn't easy to live where we did and attend the school he did when we didn't have the income the other kids' families did. The house was a remnant of my marriage. The neighbourhood was a reflection of a time when I thought there would be enough money to afford to live in it. I was just managing to hold on, but I couldn't bear moving. It was the only home Justin had ever known. I knew that if I didn't want to burst into tears again, I should focus on the task at hand. I grabbed a notepad and pen, stuffed them in my pocket, and loaded myself down with a lawn chair and my trusty blanket.

The coach was in an unusual mood that day. I was trying to put my finger on what he was attempting to display for the team. He was distracted and his approach was rather erratic. After only a few minutes of practice he called the boys to the sidelines.

"What I'm about to say isn't easy," he started. "There are some of you that just shouldn't be here. As you know, I'm filling in for the regular coach who has had surgery. I only ever expected to be the assistant, but here we are. Having said that, I really think some of you should go back to house league. I haven't seen any improvement and in a couple of cases I haven't even seen you working very hard to hold your spot. I don't have time to babysit. When you get to this level of play, I should be able to make two assumptions: you want to play and you have the ability to play. Part of my job is to assess your ability and your desire. I like winning games. I do not like losing. If losing is acceptable to you, then we have a problem. From now on, if you come to practice without the proper equipment and that includes a ball, I'm sending you home. If you come twice without your stuff, you're off the team. There are lots of boys out there who want what you've got, so if you don't want it, I don't need you."

The boys looked at each other, trying to figure out who the coach was talking to.

"Don't try and figure it out," he cautioned, "Because not one of you is exempt."

He got the boys to their feet and restarted the practice. I wanted to follow him out to the field and ask him what he had hoped to accomplish by his little 'pep' talk. I wasn't sure modeling my business acumen after this guy was such a good idea after all. Then I saw an interesting thing. The mood of the practice shifted. The boys were on point, they were focused and they were really putting forth a solid effort. The intensity of the drills increased. The level of fooling around fell off. They were taking the whole thing much more seriously. Oh sure, they still laughed and enjoyed what they were doing, but suddenly their hearts were into it, not just their bodies.

When I got in the following day, I sat my staff down at the table we use for meetings and handed out pieces of paper and pens.

"Today," I said, "We're going to take a look at how we work. Who likes having a job?"

Tentative hands rose around the table.

"Who wants to keep their job?"

The hands remained high.

"Who thinks that if keeping their jobs was dependent on how enthusiastically they did their jobs, they would still have their jobs?"

No one moved.

"Well, of course you think that. But the truth is none of us would, myself included. It's my job to look at the work that has to be done and the people I have hired to do the work. Right now, I don't see the people in the right jobs. That doesn't mean that you don't have a place, here, it's just that you might be better suited for different tasks. Comments?"

No one moved.

"Okay, then. Let's get started."

For the next couple of hours we talked about all the things that had to happen for the business to run well. Then we looked at the talents of the various people and the kind of work they liked to do. I rearranged who was doing what and tried to accommodate the demands of their lives outside of work when modifying the schedule. It seemed to work. Everyone was talking excitedly about how different things were going to be. I hoped they were right.

5

EVERY TEAM HAS ITS OWN PERSONALITY

"Coach really laid into you guys last practice," I observed over breakfast.

"We deserved it," Justin concluded.

"How so?"

"Some of the guys are lazy. And he's right; some of them shouldn't even be there."

"And you?"

"I think I deserve my spot."

"Because?"

"What's with all the questions? Don't you think I should be on the team, Mom?"

"I never said that."

"Then what? Is it costing too much money for me to play?"

"No. Where'd you come up with that?"

"Because every conversation eventually ends up with you talking about how much money we don't have."

"That's not true, Justin. The business is actually doing a bit better these days. I managed to get some cheques in so it got the bank off my bank and…"

"Because you've been stealing my coach's material."

"That's enough, Justin." I walked my bowl to the sink. I lingered at the window, looking out into the back yard wanting to be inspired by what I saw so I would know what to say to my son.

"What are you looking at?" he asked.

"Just thinking about your dad."

"I was a kid then. Don't bring him into this."

"But I have to. You brought up the topic of money. Divorces are expensive and in order to keep the house, I had to give your father a lot of money. I agree that we have had to struggle and that I probably talked too much about our finances to a kid…"

"I'm not a kid anymore, Mom."

"I know, but maybe I should have kept my concerns to myself. I just wanted you to learn how money works and that you can't spend what you don't have."

"Yeah, well Dad sure couldn't have taught me that."

"He did like to spend money. Still does, I guess, since he never has enough left for support!"

"Ouch."

"I'm sorry. He's your dad and I shouldn't..."

"It's true, he is my dad, but you don't have to watch what you say. I know what he's like. He's a jerk."

"Not always. That's what makes him so frustrating."

"Kind of like Marcus on my team. He's a really good player, but he's not consistent. Some days he never misses a shot; other days it's like his foot is allergic to the ball. You just can't count on him."

"And that effects the whole team, doesn't it?" I offered.

"Sure."

"I have that at work too. Karen's a good receptionist, but if she has had a fight with her boyfriend, she's nasty. I try to tell her that she can't take her personal problems out on us at work. She has to learn to leave that stuff at the door. I'm glad to talk to her about it, but after a while it gets kind of tiring."

"Fire her."

"Oh sure, Mr. Compassion. It's not that easy and besides, I'll just have to hire someone else with their own stuff. Then you add their stuff to everyone else's stuff...it can be a full time job just navigating that."

"So why do it?"

"Do what?" I asked as I returned to the table to finish my coffee.

"Put up with it. Is having your own business really worth the headaches?"

"Good question. And some days the answer is no. But more days, the answer is yes. I opened my business to help people. So if that means that some of the people I help are my own staff, then I guess I'm doing what I went into business to do."

"But they don't pay you."

"Not with money. But if they feel good about themselves, then they feel better about the work."

"So you help them because you're selfish?"

"Maybe a little," I smiled.

As I walked into the office that morning, I realized that Justin was right. I was selfish. I had to be. If my business was to grow, I had to nurture those who could help me. I looked around at the people who were busying themselves with getting their day started. Each one of them had their own story.

Karen was a young woman who was still finding her way to adulthood. She had started college and dropped out. She had had a string of boyfriends who weren't good for her, but she didn't want to hear that she could do better. She was moody and temperamental, but I knew she wanted to get herself settled. She dropped herself in her chair, nursing a hot chocolate and I knew that today was going to be a challenge for her and therefore the rest of us.

Drew kept his head down and checked the appointment book. He was methodical and emotionally flat. He took excellent care of his clients, but didn't spend much time conversing with the rest of us. Come to think of it, I didn't really know much about him. He had arrived at the door with solid references and I needed a chef, so that had been that. He rolled his eyes toward the ceiling whenever Karen attempted to engage him in small talk.

Missy was my part timer. She came in after school to catch up on the filing and generally picked up after the rest of us. She had expressed an interest in pursuing a career in catering and so I had taken her on to give her some experience and to relieve myself of the more mundane aspects of the business. The truth was, though, as I thought about it, without her we didn't run as smoothly. When she was sick or had a school conflict, I really missed her. She brought a certain bounce to the day. And I always thought she had a crush on Justin so she worked extra hard to impress me.

Jenn was a bit of a wild card. I wasn't sure that I had needed someone to book the "talent", but she convinced me to give her a try. She brought a small number of clients with her that added bodies to my database and I had been moved by her story. She was a single mom like myself with two little kids. She was a cancer survivor and she just needed a place to start over without a lot of pressure. I decided that I could help with that. I knew she was struggling, so I said yes.

I realized that there were a lot of gaps in my information about the people I spent hours with every single day. How could I be an effective employer when I knew so little about those who I depended on to help me run my business? And then it hit me. I couldn't understand the personality of my team until I understood the personalities of all the players and the one I had to start with was me!

I sequestered myself in my office and booted up the computer. I went on line and took as many personality tests as I could find. I examined my likes and dislikes, my work preferences, my daily habits, my problem solving models, my decision making models, my conflict resolution style – you name it, I assessed it. When I had accumulated a stack of paper almost a foot thick, I realized that there was a consistent pattern to the information I had. After that much effort and trees sacrificed, I had to accept certain things about myself to be true. Now the real work could begin.

6

KNOW ALL THE POSITIONS, BUT ONLY PLAY YOUR OWN

Justin wandered by my room on his way to the bathroom.

"Isn't it a little late for you to be up?" he asked.

"Don't ask."

He lingered at the door, "What are you working on?"

"I'm trying to balance the books for the month."

"Problems?"

"Not really. I just hate doing it. I wish I could let someone else handle it, but that hasn't worked out so good."

"Why not?"

"I have a cashflow situation. I should have been watching more closely; so I took the job of bookkeeping back. I wish I hadn't. I really do hate it."

"I get that." Justin turned from the door. "Well, see you in the morning."

I wished it was that easy for me to just change the subject and move on.

That afternoon at practice I talked to the coach about focusing on the different positions on the team and how each player made their own unique contribution. I tried to figure out the role each of my staff played in the success of the business and whether or not I really understood what they did. I never wanted to be a receptionist, but I had better understand the vital connection of that role to my overall success. Interestingly enough, the coach decided to teach the boys a lesson on that too.

"Okay," the coach began, "Today we rotate. You will never appreciate the other positions on the team if you never have an opportunity to run in their cleats." He looked over at me and nodded. Perhaps he was learning from me, too. "Defense will be my forwards, midfield play defense, and forwards take turns in net." There was general grumbling from the bench, but they knew better than to openly challenge the coach's authority.

It amazed me what I saw. The boys acted as though they had never played the game before. The defensive players got winded and stood in the middle of the field bent over, holding their sides. They couldn't take the distance they had to cover, or the rapid starts and stops. The midfields tried to run with everything they could get their feet on instead of just clearing the ball. And of course the forwards were completely stumped by having to stay put in the net. It was a circus. Patience waned and soon the otherwise easy going boys were snapping at each other and becoming increasingly verbal with their frustrations.

"Time," the coach yelled. "Come on in."

The boys didn't have to be asked twice. As they jogged to the infield, I overheard them talking with each other, sharing their appreciation for the skills of their teammates.

"How do you stay in that box? I'd go crazy just standing there, waiting for the action to come to me."

"I thought I was going to die. How do you run so much of the game?"

The coach smiled. "So, what did you learn?" he asked.

"That it sucks to be in net!" one boy called out.

"I'll take my net over what you do, every game," the net minder quipped.

Justin shifted uncomfortably. "I see that I've been a lousy teammate."

The coach looked hard at him. "What do you mean?"

"There have been a lot of times that I thought Craig was a crappy forward, but man, he runs circles around me. And when the other team scores, I blame Dillon, even though, as a defenseman, I should never let those shots get to him. I don't really know what the other guy goes through until I try it."

There were a few 'ahs' from the sillier of the boys, but generally, I think there was overwhelming agreement with what Justin said. I was proud of him.

I decided to gain that same level of understanding about all 'jobs' in my business and then to focus on what I was the best at. I recognized immediately that there were several things about running a business that I didn't much enjoy. Paper was my adversary. And Missy loved paper. I loved Missy because she took the paper from me. Missy got to stay. But then I wondered if maybe I trusted her too much. I had been allowing her to do the bank deposits on the days she came after school. Maybe it was too much to expect of a young girl.

Karen seemed to be between 'men' at the moment, so her work was pretty stable. She interacted well with the clients and they always felt their events were in good hands after Karen had met with them or taken their call. As long as she directed her caring tendencies toward our clients and not men who needed saving, we would be okay.

Drew was gifted. I had never known anyone who could throw a bunch of ingredients in a bowl and have a masterpiece emerge like he could. We didn't always provide the food, but in those instances when we did, our clients were never disappointed. He was perhaps my most valuable resource and yet I couldn't recall the last nice thing I had done for him. Talking with clients wasn't his strength, but as long as either Karen or I was in the meeting during menu selection, things usually went well. He was best in the kitchen and as the server.

And then there was Jenn. I never asked about her personal life, but there was a darkness to her personality that I was sure I didn't want to anger. Some of the people she booked or brought in for referrals were a bit suspect. I knew that her ex-husband had played in a band and that she had been their agent, but beyond that, I wasn't sure what her credentials were. She hadn't proven to be the asset that I had hoped she would and she certainly didn't have the top name connections that I was led to believe she did. Of the entire team, she was my weakest link and the one I was most reluctant to fire. There was something about her that reminded me of myself. And perhaps that was my greatest weakness in business. I always put people's problems before results or my own intuitions.

If I was going to play to win then I had to learn how the different personalities of my staff affected the overall personality of the business. I could do a lot to create a business climate, or culture, as the books called it, but in the end I could only work with who I had on the team, the skills they had, and the attitudes they held.

7

PRACTICE IS BORING, BUT IT PREDICTS PERFORMANCE

I could tell when Justin woke up in the morning that he wasn't feeling well. He's not the type of kid to pretend to be sick, so when he tells me his stomach is bothering him or his head hurts, I know that I can trust him. He'd always been that way.

"You okay this morning?" I asked.

"It's nothing."

Justin moved slowly to the end of the table. "I just need to eat."

I placed the food in front of him and watched him pick at it with little enthusiasm.

"You sure you're okay?"

Justin shrugged. "It's Dad's birthday."

I had completely forgotten. Justin agonized over his father's birthday every year. The silent struggle of a child whose loyalties were in direct opposition to his experience. "Did you want to call?"

"Why?"

"Just to let him know you remembered."

"Like he remembers my birthday?"

"Justin."

"It's not like he cares about me."

"I'm not having this conversation with your father; I'm having it with you. If you want to call, then you call."

"I don't know."

Perhaps a change of subject would bring some relief.

"What time's practice tonight?"

"Why do you do that?"

"Do what?"

"Change the subject so I'm not upset. You always do that. I'm not four anymore, Mom. You can't protect me from everything."

"I know," I whispered, "but it's what I do."

"Well, stop. It didn't help when he lived here and it doesn't help now."

I knew that saying I'm sorry wasn't going to change anything so I simply went about my routine. After a few minutes Justin left the room and I heard him making the call.

Things didn't improve when Justin arrived home for dinner. He tossed his soccer bag in the corner and walked silently to his room. I approached with caution and tapped lightly on the door. Nothing. I tapped again, a little harder.

"I heard you the first time."

"So why didn't you answer?"

"I didn't want to."

"Nice. Open the door."

"You open it. You're closer."

I had a hard time resisting my reaction. I wanted to blast through the door, screaming insubordination and disrespect, but I didn't. One thing I had to learn was how to have feelings without wildly unleashing them on the unsuspecting, although deserving, masses.

I opened the door.

"You okay?"

"Work sucks. I quit."

Shocked, I repeated what I had heard, "You quit?"

"The boss was lame. I don't need it."

"Yes, actually, you do. If you want to go to soccer camp."

"I'll get another job, then."

"What happened?"

"I don't want to talk about it."

"I do. Did you really quit?"

Justin looked horrified. "Do you think I got fired?"

That thought hadn't actually occurred to me. "No."

"Yes, I quit."

"But Justin that doesn't make any sense."

"Can't help ya."

"I want you to go and ask for your job back."

"What?"

"You heard me."

"No way. I won't."

"I'm not asking."

"You don't even know what happened. You don't know anything. You just want the money."

"That's not true."

"Whatever."

Justin blew past me in the doorway. I heard him pick up the phone and ask one of his buddies for a ride to practice.

I was waiting in the livingroom when he got home.

"So, how was practice?"

"Stupid."

"Stupid?"

"And boring. I don't see the point. It's the same exercises. We run the same drills. We have no plays. We're going to get killed this year. "

"It takes a while," I commented, attempting to sound wise and encouraging, but still wanting to rip his head off.

"You are so lame. I know what you're trying to do. Just say it."

"Say what?"

"That I was rude."

"It would appear you know that, so why would I tell you?"

"Don't pull that psychobabble crap on me. I see through it."

"And what is it you see?"

"A bitter middle aged divorcee trying to keep it together."

"And what are you trying to do, besides complain and blame me?"

"Leave me alone."

"No, really, I want to know. You've given me nothing but attitude since this morning. I want to understand."

"You can't." Justin sunk deeper into the chair beside me. I knew the best way to handle this was to wait him out, so I waited. I thought I would probably have to spend the night on the sofa since Justin appeared to be more headstrong than I had given him credit for. "You gonna stare at me all night?"

"If I have to." More silence.

"How come the kids who never come to practice still get to play?"

I wasn't expecting this change of direction. That was my signature move, not Justin's.

"Because they're on the team."

"Getting on the team isn't everything. You have to earn your spot; you know, make the coaches glad they picked you. Some guys just show up for the games. That's easy. Anybody can do that. But where are they when the rest of us are out there freezing our nuts off and doing the same drills for the fiftieth time? The coach said he wasn't going to let that happen. Remember? You were there. He said there were lots of other kids who would take the spots, but he hasn't done what he said. It makes me mad."

"I see that."

"The coach says that the practices will predict our performance. So if only half the team shows up, then we'll only be half as good as a team, right?"

"Makes sense."

"So we pay for the choices they make."

"Afraid so."

"I hate him."

"Your coach?"

"Dad."

"What's he...?"

"He didn't want to put in the work...the phone's been disconnected...can you leave me alone, now?"

I didn't say anything. So that's what this was all about. My own frustrations disappeared in the flood of my son's. Practice predicts performance and some people never attend practices. It was a lesson from the soccer pitch that mirrored life. I was sorry that his father had disappointed him, again. That his legacy with Justin would be one strewn with broken promises and hurt feelings. Some team members just don't deserve to be on the team.

Justin eventually made his way to bed. I stood at the door and watched him sleep. He had been through a lot for a kid. And he was still a kid; on the cusp of manhood, but not there yet. He still struggled with himself and who he wanted to be. It was tough being both parents. I knew nothing about boys. I only had one sister. My father sure wasn't around much when I was growing up. I had very little experience with boyfriends. My marriage had failed. And I thought I could raise a boy on my own. What was I thinking? I said a quick prayer for both of us before I headed to bed.

8

PLAY YOUR OWN GAME

I had to consider the possibility. Perhaps I was in the wrong business. What would happen if one day I woke up and realized that all my efforts had been pointless because I was never intended to do what I'm doing. What if I should have been doing something else all along? It was this thought that pinned me to my bed in fright one early morning. I laid there considering, for perhaps the twentieth time, the reasons that I had started the business that I had. It really had been more of a hobby upgrade than anything else.

I had been encouraging Justin to find a way to play his own game. I told him not to be intimidated by his team mates who had been playing regional longer than he had. I suggested that he find his own place and make the contribution that only he could make. So why couldn't I follow my own advice?

I grabbed the pen and paper that I kept on my nightstand. I began the SWOT analysis that I had used on my business, only this time applied it to myself. What were my personal strengths? What were my personal weaknesses? How could I use my strengths to build a business? And how could I manage my weaknesses to minimize the threats they posed?

I asked myself what the values were for my life and how building a business supported them. It was a very uncomfortable time. I wasn't sure I wanted to know the answers to the questions I was posing. My responses could inflict a great deal of change on a woman whose level of comfort with change was quite low. And what about Justin? Hadn't I brought enough chaos into his world? Wasn't I the reason that he was struggling with so many things?

As the alarm buzzed, I was left with more questions than time to consider them. Resorting to a familiar pattern of coping, I turned the thinking off and mechanically began my day.

"You look like crap," Justin commented as he passed me in the hall.

"Feel the same way," I countered.

"A woman your age should get more rest," he offered.

"And a boy your age should know better than to point that out."

He smiled and strolled away from me. He really was a good kid.

"So, how's business?" he asked over his cereal.

"Funny you should ask."

He looked a little nervous. "Something wrong?"

"Not really. I've just been wondering if I'm in the right business."

"Navel contemplation time?"

"No. You know I'm not that philosophical. I've just been thinking…"

"Is this going to be one of those long conversations, because I've got a test first period."

Lost in my thoughts, I didn't pay much attention to his comment.

"You know how I've been telling you to play your own game?"

He nodded.

"Well, I'm thinking I should play my own game, too."

"What does that mean?"

"I want to be excited about what I do. I want to make a difference. I just don't feel like I'm doing that right now. I want to make sure it's just a phase, and not a misguided effort."

"So, how will you know?"

"That's where I get stuck."

"My coach tells us to remember the love of the game. If we don't love it any more, then we should be doing something else. Do you love your business, Mom?"

"Not like I love you," I joked.

"Don't do that. I'm trying to help. You want to talk to me like I'm another adult, but when I offer a suggestion you treat me like a kid again. You can't have it both ways."

He was right. And in this moment, perhaps being more of an adult than I was.

"Sorry. To answer your question. No. I don't love it. I don't even like it any more."

"Then do something else."

"I wish it was that simple."

"It is. You just don't want to see it. Quit making up excuses."

Was I? I wanted to consider the possibility. I picked up the phone and dialed the office. I waited for the machine to pick up. "Good morning everyone. It's me. I just wanted to let you know that I'm taking the day off for strategic planning. You won't be able to reach me. So if something comes up, handle it and let me know what you did. I trust you. Have a good time." I hung up the phone, already regretting what I had done. What would I do now that I had committed to reconsidering my options? What if I did discover that I hated my work life? Too much thinking. I'd just go to the Coffee House and drink caffeine for a while. That would help.

I entered just as the morning rush of customers was thinning. I sat at a booth that looked out onto the intersection. I watched cars and people scurrying in every direction. I knew how they felt. I wondered if they had any better sense of life direction than I did. I was so absorbed in my thoughts that I didn't hear Lucy come by and sit across from me.

"Hey stranger," she said.

I nearly jumped through the glass window. "What are you doing sneaking up on me like that?"

"I didn't sneak. You were off in your own little world. Don't blame me for your lack of attention."

Lucy and I had known each other a long time. We had been through a lot. It sometimes seemed like we were living parallel lives. Our kids were the same age and we often joked how cool it would be if they ended up marrying each other. But remembering how unsuccessfully we had chosen our own partners, we thought we should leave those types of decisions up to them.

"So, what's going on?" Lucy asked. "And why aren't you at work already?"

"I'm taking the morning off. Maybe the whole day. I need time to think."

"I heard."

"Heard?"

"About Justin."

I was numb. Was there more to the job story than I knew? Were my suspicions right?

"And?" I was hoping to draw her out without having to confess that I didn't what to know what she was talking about.

"Well, I was surprised when Abbi told me he was going. Where is he getting the money?" Panic set in.

"Going?"

"Summer soccer camp."

"I knew about that. He has been working here part time to save the money."

"Here?"

"Yes."

"I don't think so."

"Lucy, I think I know where my son is working."

Just then the owner strolled by the table. "Hey, Peter. Do you have a minute?"

"Sure. What's up?"

"It's my son, Justin and his job."

"Oh, yeah. He came in here a few weeks back for a job. Told him I didn't have anything but to check back. Never saw him again. Is he still looking?"

There was no way to hide to my reaction. "I don't know," I confessed more to myself than him.

I looked at Lucy.

"I told you," she said. "So where is he getting the money? Is Jim helping him out?"

I shook my head.

"You okay?" I stood up and walked out. So much for my thinking time.

9

DON'T BE SCARED…KICK THE BALL!

The reality is, I didn't know what to do. I wasn't sure how to talk to Justin and I wasn't sure I wanted to. It was just like my marriage and just like my business. If I ignored the problem, maybe it would go away. Of course, I knew how that strategy had worked out in the past and I wasn't prepared to fool myself again.

I had problems. They were everywhere. I had never felt so alone. I couldn't go to work – I had told them I was taking the day to build a better future. I couldn't go home – Justin might already be there on his lunch break. I wandered around and eventually found myself in our church. I sat in the front pew and dropped myself down. I felt like I weighed 400 pounds. And that was just my heart!

I had been struggling and fighting to build a life for the two of us for so long that I hadn't considered that I had been doing the wrong things. My son was keeping something from me. Maybe more than one thing. How could I live with him and miss that he had changed? I admit that I had been preoccupied with the business lately. I had been focused more on my own stuff. He was a young man. Surely I didn't need to parent him as much as I had in the past. Why was everything in my life so draining?

Realizing that I was focused more on my problems than on creating solutions, I tried to shift my thinking to something more positive. I failed. I couldn't get past the fact that my life was not what I had been trying to create. Something had happened. Something had gone wrong and I had no clue what it was.

I found my way home around 4 o'clock. Justin was there. I could tell because his shoes were tossed carelessly at the door and the contents of his lunch bag were strewn across the counter.

"Where have you been?" he asked from his desk.

"Around."

"You okay?"

"What reason do I have not to be?" I challenged. Of course it wasn't a challenge, because he had no clue what I was talking about.

"You just don't seem yourself."

"What time's practice?"

"Same time as every other Tuesday since the season began."

"Yeah, well things change," I snapped.

"Like you?"

"Sure. Just like me." I went in to my room, closed the door and cried. Cried softly though, so Justin didn't hear.

At practice that night, I got a lesson about communication. It wasn't supposed to be. It was actually a drill on kicking the ball.

"What is your problem?" the coach bellowed from the sidelines. "Kick the ball! We don't score unless someone kicks the ball. Talk to each other and KICK THE BALL!"

I thought about that. No one was saying anything. There was no way to know where the other guys were or who was available to receive the pass. If they continued to stay quiet, nothing was going to improve. Interesting how life was mimicking sport. I had to start talking. I owed it to my staff and to my son. Mostly my son. It wasn't going to be an easy conversation. But then, not having it was tearing me apart too, so it was a matter of which torment I preferred.

10

DON'T MISS THE EASY SHOTS

"You got a minute?" I asked Justin after he had showered.

"I still have homework."

"It'll just take a minute."

"Okay. Just let me throw on some shorts."

I had no idea what I was doing. How do I ask my son where the money was coming from? Was he dealing drugs? Did he steal from kids at school? A thousand things raced through my mind. And sadly, I was just as concerned about my role in creating a criminal as I was about his demise. Selfish.

"What's up, Mom?"

"Come, sit down."

"Now you're just being weird. What's wrong?"

"What do you do all day when I'm at work?"

"School." Then, almost as an afterthought, "And I used to have my job."

"But it's almost summer. What do you plan to do with yourself?"

"The usual. Just hang out."

"Have you done anything about getting your job back?"

"I already have a job," he offered brightly.

Yes, of course, that was it. He had another job! Why hadn't I thought of that?

"You do?"

"Sure. Being a great son is a full time job."

My heart sunk. No reprieve as hoped. I had to redirect.

"Do you have anything you want to tell me?" How likely was it that he was going to confess to robbing a bank for soccer camp or that he had intentionally lied about the job?

"No."

Now what?

"You would tell me wouldn't you, if something was wrong?"

"Not if you were all weird like you are right now. What's wrong, Mom? Has Dad done something?"

"No. Not at all. This is about you."

"Have I done something?"

"Justin…" I hesitated. I couldn't do it. I couldn't just ask him straight up how he was able to afford his camp fee. I couldn't take the easy shot.

I had heard the coach tell the boys to keep it simple, to take the easy shots when they were available. I saw the confusion on Justin's face. Why couldn't I talk to my son? When had the stakes gotten so high that I couldn't just be his mother?

"Were you going to finish that sentence any time soon?"

I had to take the shot.

"Justin, I bumped into Lucy today. She asked me something interesting."

I watched for some tell tale sign from my son, but he didn't even flinch.

"She wanted to know if Jim was helping you pay for summer camp."

Justin didn't even blink. He stared at me with eyes of steel. "And what did you say?"

His nerve rattled me. He was so calm. "I told her the truth. I said that you had a part time job at the Coffee House. That you were paying."

Nothing.

"Imagine my surprise when Peter came along and asked why you hadn't been back."

"So that's what this whole heart to heart has been about, setting me up?"

"I'm not the one lying here."

"So now I'm a liar? I'm outa here." He started to walk away.

"Get back here," I said with more force than I intended.

"Why? You've already made up your mind about me." He turned, then stopped. He spun to face me again and hissed. "You're right, I don't work at the Coffee House. I never did. But I knew that if I came home and told you that, you would freak. I just can't handle another bout of controlling parent, right now."

The slamming door was the last thing I heard before I dissolved into tears on the couch.

11

COACHES HAVE TO BE ABLE TO DEMONSTRATE THE SKILLS FOR THE GAME

I don't know what time I fell asleep, I just know that when I woke up, Justin had already left. I heard the back door slam shut. How quickly our relationship had deteriorated. I moved through my morning routine in a fog.

I turned off the ceiling fan in my room and slowly threw the comforter across the bed. I would have given anything to be able to crawl back under it and pull the covers over my head. Bury myself in down. But that wasn't going to happen.

It was a new month. I had to face the bleak task of reconciling bank statements and assessing the general financial ill health of the business. It was June. It was the half way mark. All indicators would probably point down.

That was encouraging. I was certainly in a good mood this morning. My son hated me. I hated my business. It was absolutely delightful being me today.

I found my way to my desk; just in time to drop my head on it and start to sob. I heard a soft knock.

"You okay?" Jenn poked her head in.

"Not really." I answered.

She came in, closed the door behind her and dropped in the chair. "Men or money?"

"Yes," I answered.

"I hear ya and I don't mean to add to an already lousy day, but I have another job. Friday is my last day."

Well, she was direct if nothing else.

"I see. Anyone I know?"

"I'm getting back together with my ex. His band is going on the road and he wants me to be there."

"But isn't that where the trouble started for you two?"

"He's changed. I can see it. And we have the kids now. Things will be okay."

"You're taking the children on the road with you?"

"Sure, all the big names do it, all the time."

"I didn't realize your husband was a 'big name'." I shouldn't have said that, but it was too late.

"I thought you'd be happy for me, but I guess everyone's right. You're so full of your own issues, there isn't any room for you to think of the rest of us."

I was shocked. Who was saying these things? And what made them think I had issues?

"I am happy for you, Jenn, if you're sure this is what you want."

"It is. I have a chance to get my life back on track before it's too late."

What was she implying? Was it too late for me? Had everyone been talking about that too? I had no fight left in me. "I wish you well. I'll be sorry to see you leave, but I want the best for you."

I put on my best game face for the rest of the day. I had to appear happy and yet every time I looked at my staff I wondered who was saying what about me behind my back. I set about the business of running my business with a renewed fury. It was obvious I couldn't count on anyone else to help me. I had to do it alone. Like everything in my life. If it could be difficult, I would find a way to make it more difficult. If it could be easy, I could still find a way to make it difficult. I felt very alone as I ploughed through the work. I was a woman on a mission. Tragic that I didn't have a clue what it was.

"You ready to take me to practice?"

"I won't be staying tonight."

"Why not?"

"I think I made a mistake. There isn't really anything I can learn from your coach."

"Since when?"

"Jenn quit today."

"And these two things are related how?"

"It's not working."

"Could you maybe say what you're talking about? I'm confused."

"I'm trying to do the things the coach tells you. It's really good stuff, but I just can't seem to get it together. My staff is talking about me behind my back. I'm not making any money. Jenn thinks it's better to follow her cheating, lying, drug-taking husband around on the road as a groupie manager than work for me…. How sad is that?" whispering, I added, "I just don't get it. And on top of all that, my son thinks he has no choice but to lie to me about having a job. I haven't forgotten about that, Justin. You owe me an explanation."

"I didn't want to disappoint you. You've got so much going on right now."

Justin went to practice without saying another word. No coaxing. No teasing. Nothing. I was still sitting on the couch when he got back.

"How was practice?"

"You don't care, remember?"

"I care."

He came and plopped down beside me. "You stink," I told him as though he wasn't aware of that for himself.

"That's what happens when you work hard on something important." I could have almost predicted the next words out of his mouth. "When was the last time you broke a sweat?" I ignored the question. "You should have been there tonight."

"Why is that?"

"You would have gotten to see coach play. He's got some moves."

"Oh yeah. Like what?"

"The nutmeg…he even deeked out Chris. He said it was time to let us see that he knew the game. That he had skill too. Then he showed us."

I thought for a minute. The coach really did know the game and he had the skills to play it. He was teaching the boys to first trust, and then he would bring the evidence. I couldn't help myself. I started to apply that lesson to my business. Did I instill trust in my employees? Did I bring the proof that I knew what I was doing? Was what I was doing the best use of my skills? More questions than answers again. At least I was getting used to living with ambiguity.

12

FIND A ROLE MODEL WORTH MODELING

"Coach says now that school is over, he will be giving us homework."

The team had been together for a little more than six weeks. They had played two games, tied one and lost one. The coach was frustrated. The boys were frustrated. They needed something. I guess the coach thought homework was the place to start.

"Like what?"

"Well, it's kind of a no brainer. We have to watch at least one game a week on TV. Pros. We have to watch our position on the team and see what they do that we don't. He's going to pick the game and we all have to watch the same one, so we're all talking about the same thing."

"That makes sense. Anything else?"

"We have to find a role model."

"Did he give any suggestions?"

"No. He wants us to choose a soccer player we admire and learn as much as we can about him."

"Who are you going to choose?"

"I'm not sure yet. Maybe Rooney."

"Oh yeah. Why him?"

"He's got talent."

"Do you think that's all it takes to be successful?"

"No," then he added with a grin, "but it's a great place to start."

I laughed. He had a point.

"Why don't you do it with me?"

"Do what?"

"Choose a role model."

"Last time I checked, I wasn't on the team."

"No, but you are struggling to run your business. Why not find someone who's already successful and do what they did? If it works for soccer, wouldn't it work for you too?"

I hated it when he was smarter than me. "I suppose it would."

"So, who would you choose?"

"I'm not sure. I'll have to think about it for a while."

"It's due Thursday before the game." He turned to walk toward the bathroom.

Thinking about my business role model really challenged me. I realized that I didn't really know that many business owners, let alone ones that I wanted to emulate. It started to dawn on me that not having someone to talk to about the business might be hurting my chances of being successful. How would I know what success looked like for myself if I didn't recognize it in others?

I decided to start with who I knew, and I knew Peter. He had owned the local coffee shop for as long as we had lived in the area. He was always friendly and I guess by virtue of the fact that he had been around forever, he must be doing something right.

I waited at the counter, sipping my coffee, until the morning rush was over. As I watched the last patron scurry out, I realized that I didn't have a clue what I was going to talk to him about. I should have gotten better instructions from Justin – or thought it through myself a little more.

"Hey, Peter," I ventured, "could I talk to you for a few minutes?"

He turned from the shelves with a curious look on his face. "Something wrong?"

"Yep."

"The coffee too strong this morning?"

"No. Nothing's wrong with the coffee." I could see the look of relief. "I have a business of my own and it's not going very well these days. I was hoping I could get a little advice."

"Nope."

I was crushed. "Oh. Okay." I quickly buried my warming face in the coffee mug.

"Advice would mean I knew what would fix your problems. I got enough of my own problems to fix." This wasn't getting any better. "What I will do is grab a coffee and sit down with you to talk about both our businesses." I started to brighten. "You gave up too easy. Maybe that's what you're doing at your work, too." He took a mug off the shelf, confidently swung the coffee pot, first to fill himself, then to top me up. "Deal?"

I grinned. "Deal."

Peter and I talked like old friends. He asked me about my struggles, my triumphs, my family, and my friends. We had been visiting for almost an hour, and still nothing about the business. I was getting a little frustrated with my choice of mentors.

"So," I directed, "when would you like to talk about business?"

His answer threw me. "I have been."

"We have?"

"Sure. What is business if it isn't making money being ourselves?"

I was so lost.

"I can't know anything about your business if I don't know you. That's just the way it is." He got up to put on another pot of coffee. The break crowd would soon be arriving and I was sure it was his subtle way of letting me know our conversation was ending.

"Well, I better be getting on my way."

When he turned to face me, he looked baffled and bewildered.

"Why?"

"Won't you be getting busy again soon?"

"Hopefully, but that doesn't mean you have to go. In fact, I insist you stay. Maybe you'll understand better if you watch it happen."

"Watch what?"

"Relationships."

Peter was right. He knew how to connect with people. He might have been selling coffee, but he was most definitely a therapist. It was amazing to watch him work. He really knew these people. I thought about my clients and remembered that I didn't even really know my staff, let alone my customers. How pathetic. Business was about the people and understanding them. After the crowd thinned again, I told Peter what I had seen. He smiled and then grew solemn.

"But you didn't get the first piece. Before you can build relationships with your customers, you have to have a strong relationship with someone else."

I was excited. I knew the answer to this one. "Right. My staff."

"No."

"No?"

"First you have to know yourself. That's where it all starts. So if you want to talk to me again about your business, you have to figure yourself out. Get to know yourself. What you like. What you don't like. What gets you out of bed in the morning, or pins you to sheets with terror. You gotta know this stuff before you throw yourself into the marketplace.

Otherwise, you'll never have an anchor or foundation to build on. Now, get out of my shop and go find yourself."

He turned abruptly and walked to the back. There I was, alone with a stranger - myself.

"So," Justin asked, "have you found yourself a mentor?"

"I think so."

"Who is it?"

"Peter."

"From the Coffee Hause?"

"That's the one."

Justin looked uneasy. I'm sure he thought I was going to bring the job up again. I didn't. He knew what was expected of him if he wanted to go to soccer camp. His life lesson was to learn to be responsible and do what was required of him. As far as I knew, he was either working or not going to camp. End of discussion. Maybe he needed to look in the mirror, too, and decide whether he liked what he saw or not.

13

As skill develops, add more challenges

"Have you noticed how the drills are getting tougher?" the coach asked the boys as they sauntered back to the bench.

There were moans and groans from his players.

"Why is that?" he asked.

"You hate us?"

"You're trying to kill us?"

"You're punishing us for losing last week?"

"All good reasons," he replied smiling, "but none of them the right reason. The drills are getting harder because you are getting better."

"You're kidding, right?" Mitch asked.

"Not at all. Imagine if, when you were babies, your parents had been content with letting you crawl. You guys would look pretty ridiculous out on the field on all fours wouldn't you?" His comment and question were met with chuckles. "If no one challenges us, we accept our current level of performance as the best we can do. Our current level of performance is RARELY the best we can do. I have to push you to the next level. It's my job. Now, let's get back out there. Speed drills are next."

I watched the boys as they bristled. They hated the speed drills. Yet speed drills were exactly what the boys needed. They were good, but they weren't as fast as their competition. They had to work on what they least wanted to work on. Just like the assignment I had been given by Peter. It was what I needed to do to compete, but I was reluctant to look inside. I was scared. I hadn't done anything close to self-reflection for years. What if I didn't like what I found? Or worse yet, what if there wasn't anything TO find?

"You look distracted, Mom. What's up?" Justin asked as we walked back to the car after practice.

"How do you make yourself do the drills?"

"Coach's wrath."

"That's the only reason?"

"Sometimes. I just don't want him to get mad at us. It's worse when he's mad."

"Is that a good enough reason?"

"What difference? It works." Justin threw his bag in the back of the car.

I thought about what he said as we drove home. Sometimes you just have to find the motivation, right or wrong, to get things done. I knew I had to do what Peter told me to do if

I wanted to go back and talk to him again. Intellectually, it was the right thing to do. But I hadn't done it. I wanted to understand why. My business depended on my accomplishing the 'drill' he had given me. Maybe I didn't have the skill. Maybe I wasn't ready. Peter should have known it was too hard. What kind of a coach was he? And then it hit me. He was the best kind. He was encouraging me to walk instead of crawl. Talking to him was easy. But now he was asking me to talk to myself and that was a much more terrifying conversation.

"What are you thinking about, Mom?"

"The drills. I think I may have stalled at the easy ones. Do you remember telling me to get a mentor?"

"Yeah."

"Well, I did. I talked to Peter at the coffee shop around the corner."

"That's cool. How did it go?"

"Pretty good."

"But?"

"Well he said some things I don't really understand."

"Can I help?"

"He told me to figure out who I was and what I wanted."

"Sounds tough."

"It's been a long time since I even considered I had the right to ask."

"Because of Dad?"

I smiled. "No. I can't blame him for everything."

"Why then?"

"I don't know. I guess I just thought once I made certain choices, I couldn't change my mind."

"That's dumb. We get to change our minds all the time."

"How did you get so smart?"

"Watching you screw up."

"Very funny."

After feeding Justin, I decided to spend a few minutes in a hot tub contemplating life. I closed my eyes tightly and tried to remember what it was like to be me before I gave so many pieces of myself away.

I tried to remember what I did as a kid. The kinds of games I liked to play, the toys I preferred, the books I read, and the friends I told my deepest secrets to. I had flashes of memories, but the harder I tried to remember the sadder I got. I couldn't connect to anything that sparked the type of fire in the belly I was hoping this exercise would. It left me deflated and wondering whether or not Peter had wasted his time.

"It's basics first, Mom." Justin offered. "You're trying to win the World Cup, but you're still in house league. You have to pace yourself. You can't expect to never think about this stuff and then have all the answers just because you want to. You might actually have to work at it."

"Now, you're my coach?"

"Recognize talent when it's in front of you, I always say."

"You never say that." I reached and ruffled the top of his hair. He was a decent kid after all. I must have been

71

doing something right and the rest of it would all work out eventually.

14

DON'T TAKE YOUR EYE OFF THE BALL

The next day at work I realized how important it is to pay attention to your business. When I arrived, there was chaos.

"Jenn's gone."

"Not for two weeks." I answered.

"No. She's gone. Friday was her last day. You knew that. And took all her files with her."

"Why would she do that?" I asked.

"Because maybe she lied to you," Drew shrieked.

The thought had never crossed my mind. "Lied to me?" I whispered.

"I heard her talking on the phone to that loser husband of hers. She said she was going to take all the client files with her and they could start to build their business off your sweat."

"But she said…"

"People say a lot of things, boss. Mostly, they lie if it serves them."

I didn't know what to say. I didn't know where to start. I knew what Jenn did, but I trusted her to manage her own events and clients. My clients and my events, I mean. I had taken my eye off the ball and it had been snatched away from me.

"So what are you going to do?" Drew pressed me for an answer I didn't have.

"I have to think."

"Well don't take too long."

I stumbled out the door, down the street, and found myself standing outside Peter's coffee shop. I couldn't go in. I hadn't done my homework. But I had nowhere else to go.

"You gonna stand there staring or come in?" Peter asked from behind.

I jumped. "I didn't see you there."

"Or hear me either, I guess. I had to call you three times before I got your attention."

"Sorry."

"What happened?"

"I'm kind of lost."

"What happened?"

"I trusted someone who shouldn't have been trusted."

"Sounds about right." He walked around the counter. "Did you do what I told you to?"

"I tried."

"Handy excuse for failure."

"It's not easy, you know."

"At what point did I say it would be?"

"I expected to know something about myself that would be useful."

"Why does it have to have a purpose? Can't knowing yourself be enough?"

"But you said…"

"I just said you had to know yourself before you could go to market. What you do with what you learn is up to you, but the discovery process is just that – a process. The content of what you learn should be valuable for its own sake. Unless you don't think you're valuable."

"I'm not really in the mood for psychobabble, Peter. My entertainment coordinator just ran off with all my client files. My problems are a little more immediate than getting to know myself better."

"Are you always so resistant to help?"

I stared at him.

"Maybe I don't blame her for leaving you. Or screwing you in the process." He walked to the back of the shop.

"I came here for help," I called out after him.

"No you didn't," he snapped back. "You came for sympathy and I sold my last serving ten minutes ago. Get out."

"I beg your pardon?"

"I said get out. I have nothing for you until you do what you're told." I heard him slam the door to his office and although I sat at the counter for almost two hours, he never came to my rescue.

When I returned to the office, bedlam had unleashed itself.

"Where have you been?" Drew screamed.

"Thinking."

"Well while you were doing that, two clients called to find out why Jenn is trying to rebook their event with her and four others called to say they had decided to go with Jenn because they think she's the brains of the business anyway. So, I hope whatever you were thinking about, Einstein, it contains a way to keep this business open."

I couldn't even look at him. "I took my eye off the ball."

"What?"

"I took my eye off the ball and she stole it from me."

"So what does that mean?"

"I have to get the ball back. We have to go back to basic drills. Speed and accuracy. The quality of the shot."

"Have you lost your mind?"

"What business are we in?"

"I'm not talking to you anymore. You're nuts."

"No. Bear with me. What business are we in?"

"Catering."

"No. That's what you do. What business are we in?"

"Entertainment?"

"Not anymore," I quipped.

"Event planning."

"Closer. That's what I do."

"So, I don't understand."

"If we can get back to our core business, maybe we can salvage what Jenn has tried to take."

"She hasn't tried, boss. She has taken it."

"Drew, you're missing the point. She has names. Contacts. But she doesn't have us. She can't do what we do. It's why she will fail. She isn't a chef, is she?" Drew shook his head. "She doesn't know what I do to pull it all together in the back room when no one else is here. She never wanted to learn and I never felt that I could trust her enough to show her. She only has a list of impersonal information. We have the relationships, Drew. We are the ones the clients work with."

"But we're losing clients. They've been calling."

"Like who?"

"The Dressers."

"They never paid their bill on time and they were very difficult to work with. We're better off without them. Who else?"

He looked through the phone messages. "The Parkers. They throw a summer party every year that brings a lot of referral business."

"They'll be back. And so will their referrals."

"How can you be so sure?"

"Because Jenn doesn't know what I know about the electrical at their summer place. We'll see how loyal they are to her when she blows the circuits and the air conditioning goes out and the dips are served room temperature. Drew, this is a setback. I'm not going to lie to you, but I can't follow you down the road of total destruction. We'll be fine."

"I don't get it."

"You just have to have a little faith." My calmness shocked me. I had no idea whether I could take my own advice, but I did know that he needed to hear it and as his boss, he needed to hear it from me. "You're a great employee, Drew. I appreciate how emotional you are about our future. Thanks."

He shook his head and left the office. I had been stable and sure. I had been reassuring and gentle. Maybe I was starting to see what Peter had hoped I would. Maybe it wasn't about the usefulness of the quality, but the recognition of it that mattered first.

I may have taken my eye off the ball briefly, but it wouldn't happen again.

"Justin," I called as I came in the back door.

"Yeah."

"Can you come here, please?"

He sauntered from his room.

"I haven't noticed you heading off to work." Breaking my own rule, not to ask, I decided that I wasn't taking my eye of this ball, either.

"I haven't been able to find anything."

"Well, then I want you to start again tomorrow morning. There must be something out there. I want you to find it."

"But Mom."

"Nope. I was going to stay out of it, but you insist that there is nothing more important to you than soccer and this summer camp, so I have to make sure you go."

"Camp's in two weeks. I can never make enough in two weeks…"

"Especially if you are still sitting in your room feeling sorry for yourself."

"What do you suggest I do?"

"I don't know, but you have camp in two weeks, so get creative."

15

THE FIRST GAME YOU HAVE TO WIN
IS THE ONE IN YOUR HEAD

"First to the ball," the coach yelled from the sidelines. "You have to be first to the ball."

I watched in horror. Tonight was an important game. This team was undefeated. Justin was nervous. He knew they were going to be outmatched on almost all fronts. He told me that they would be killed. And so far, he was right. I watched the other team in amazement. It didn't matter where the ball went, a defender sent it out. It didn't matter where our defense kicked it, they had a midfielder or forward waiting. It seemed like they knew what our guys were thinking and were ready for it even before they did it. I couldn't tell Justin, but their team was beautiful to watch. They had it together and they knew what to do with it. But then I focused my attention on Justin's team. They never really got into the game, either. It was as though they had given up even before they took to the field. They weren't the same team. They jogged to the ball as though accepting they wouldn't be there first. Their kicking was soft and misdirected because they expected the opposing team to stop them. Their bodies were only responding to what their brains had already decided. They were going to lose. And so they did.

"So," I said, meeting Justin half way across the field. "What do you suppose happened out there tonight?"

Justin looked at me as though I had lost my mind. "We got creamed. Just like I said we would."

"So you knew you were going to lose?"

"Duh? I told you that on the way here."

"So, why even play?"

"What?"

"Well you had already decided you were going to lose, so why not just forfeit?"

"You can't do that."

"But you might as well have and saved us all the pain of watching it."

"Are you trying to help?"

"Actually, I am. Your team never had a chance tonight."

"We knew that."

"But it wasn't because the other team was better."

"They ARE better."

"But that's not why you lost. You lost because you had decided you were going to lose before you stepped onto the field."

"Is this more of your business psychobabble?"

"No. I just paid attention to what you said and what your team did. The other team was better, there is no doubt about that, but you just accepted that they would win and you never tried to stop them."

"I worked my butt off out there."

"But you left your heart on the bench."

"What?"

"Because you believed you would lose, you felt like losers, and because you felt like losers, you played like losers. So you lost."

"Let me get this. If we had believed we could beat the number one ranked, undefeated team in the league, we could have done it?"

"Don't be a brat. I'm not saying that. But what if you had used the opportunity to build your skills tonight? What if, instead of accepting the defeat before you started to play, you decided as a team you would use this opportunity to elevate your game? You get better by playing harder, more skilled teams. Anybody can boast beating a team that doesn't challenge them. Do you honestly think the other team is celebrating right now? They're probably thinking the game was a waste of their time. There wasn't any glory in that victory tonight. Scoring was merely a technicality."

"You seem to know a lot about soccer all of a sudden."

"I'm a quick learner."

"How's business?"

What a great defender. He certainly knows how to block my shots, and hit me where it hurts.

"Were we talking about business?"

"You got your nose in mine, I thought I'd return the favor."

I didn't even bother to respond. We rode the rest of the way home in silence. Just as he was about to jump out of the car, Justin spoke.

"Sorry, Mom. I know you were just trying to help me."

"Yes, I was," I answered. And said nothing else.

I went about the business of washing Justin's uniform and settling in with a good book. Justin moved around as though I was either a delicate flower or a time bomb. It didn't really matter to me which he thought I was, as long as he kept his distance until I liked being his mother again.

"I said I was sorry," he offered.

I waited. Dramatic effect. "I heard you."

"Then why aren't you talking to me?"

"It isn't as easy as saying a couple of words and expecting it to be all better. You hurt my feelings and missed the point I was trying to make."

"I know. It's just so hard. I knew we were going to get beat."

"But the final score is only part of the game, Justin."

"They're better than us. You saw that."

"Yes, I did. So, let's talk about that. What are they better at?"

"Everything."

"More specific, please."

"They pass way better."

"And how do you suppose they got better?"

"By passing?"

"Exactly. They didn't get better by conceding that other teams were already better. We could continue this exercise for every area they outplayed you, but I'm going to spare you that. Here's the bottom line: when you take away all the excuses, the only thing left is character. So, what did you learn about your character and your team's character tonight?"

"We suck?"

"No."

"We think like losers."

"Sometimes, but no. That the first game you have to win is the one in your head and when you lose that one, you will lose the one on the field. You have to believe in your ability to show up and play to your best, so even when you lose, you leave the field with dignity."

"You make it sound like a war."

"Isn't it? Isn't it a battle for first?"

"I never thought about it like that before. That's pretty cool."

"So do you want to be a foot soldier or do you want to be a general?"

"Is this another trick question?"

I smiled. It would be now.

"I have to be a foot soldier for a while," Justin began, "so I can get good in battle, then when I am a general, I understand strategy and know how to win."

I smiled again. "Right."

I saw him shift his weight. "Now, can I ask you something, Mom?"

"Of course."

"Have you won the game in your head?"

I should have seen that coming. He waited for my answer.

"Are you sure you don't play offense?"

"I want you to win your game too, Mom."

I smiled. "I know you do. I'm working on it."

"Anything I can do to help?" he offered.

"Just keep showing up in my corner."

"Deal. And Mom."

"Yes."

"I got a job today."

I grinned. I knew he could. He just had to win the game in his head.

I tossed and turned in bed that night, considering Justin's question. The truth was that I wasn't winning the game in my head. I didn't even really believe in the game anymore. And with that realization I drifted off into the best sleep I had had in several weeks.

16

WHEN THE COACH TALKS, IT IS YOUR JOB TO LISTEN

I found myself outside Peter's coffee shop. The morning crowd was thinning and I hoped that I had enough self-reflection material to satisfy him.

"You're back."

"Yep." I noticed he was struggling with the pile of cups and plates. "Something wrong?"

"I hurt my wrist."

I jumped up from the stool. "Let me help."

"Thanks," he said handing me the stack. "Would you be able to stick around and help me for a while?"

I didn't even hesitate, "Absolutely." I wasn't sure that it was the best use of my time, considering my own business was going down in flames, but how could I say no?

The next few hours passed very quickly. I cleared tables, washed dishes, put on fresh coffee, and chatted with several patrons. I laughed a lot. When I grabbed my purse to leave, I could feel my cell phone vibrating. There were 12 messages, all from Drew. I started to listen to them, but grew more and more agitated with each one. I wasn't dealing well with his heightening frenzy.

I called the office.

"Where are you?" he yelled.

"What's the problem?"

"I have the Duncans here. They want to sign their contract and I don't know where you keep that stuff. Are you interested in running this business or not?"

"I'll be right there." I had totally forgotten about the Duncans. They were on the high maintenance client list. They would not be pleased that I wasn't there. They might even cancel their event with us. It had been a bad morning to wait tables for Peter.

"I have to go," I told Peter.

"Crisis at the office?"

"Seems like it."

"Did you enjoy yourself this morning?"

I smiled, "It was fun."

"You were good. If you're ever looking for work…"

"Thanks," I called out over my shoulder.

"I can't stay at practice tonight," I told Justin over dinner. "I lost a major event this afternoon and I have to figure out how to replace the work."

"What happened?"

"I missed an appointment with the Duncans."

"So?"

"So, they didn't like that. They cancelled their event with us and they're going to book with someone else."

"Too bad."

"You could say that. Drew's furious and threatened to quit. It just wasn't a very good day all around."

"It won't be a fun practice for us either. Coach is going to kill us for the game the other night. He already warned us."

"How is that productive? You've already lost the game. Wouldn't it be better to focus on ways to improve before the next time?"

"You want to coach us?"

"Because I'm proving myself to be so effective in my own life?"

He laughed. "No. You'd just be a whole lot easier on us."

"You gotta listen to your coach, Justin. He knows the game. When he talks, it's your job to listen, especially if you want to get better."

"Why don't I call Luke and see if I can catch a ride with him?"

"That would be great. Thanks."

It was only the second practice I didn't take Justin to all season. I felt guilty. Why was it that no matter where I was, I felt like I should be somewhere else?

After thirty minutes of thinking, I grew restless. I couldn't secure new business as it was. How did I plan to recover from the Duncan situation? I decided that I needed a change of scenery.

I knocked lightly on the door. I could see the light on in the back. After the second knock, I saw Peter emerge from the kitchen.

"What are you doing here so late," I asked.

"I don't just show up when the place is open. And you?"

"Things didn't go very well today. I needed think time."

"Why are you here?"

"It seems to be where I end up these days."

"Come in and take a seat."

I unloaded my tale of woe to Peter as he leaned against the counter.

"Have you thought about what I said?" he asked.

"Yeah, but the answers aren't coming fast enough. By the time I figure things out, there may not be a business to run."

"Are you giving up?"

"Just trying to be realistic."

"Realism is overrated."

"Will you tell my banker that?"

Peter smiled and handed me a piece of paper. "If you found out you had a year to live, write down the five things you would focus on."

1. Justin

2. Justin's future

3. Reconnecting with friends and family

4. Enjoying my life

5. Finding a cure for what was killing me

"Six months?"

The same list.

"Three months?"

No changes.

"Does your business currently provide for any of those five things?"

"Not really."

"Then get out of it." He could tell by the look on my face that getting out wasn't really an option at the moment. "Then stay in."

"That doesn't solve anything either."

"Then what do you want?"

I looked around and what I said next really surprised me. "I want this."

What Peter said next, surprised me even more. "Good. It's yours. When you're ready to take over, come and see me. We'll figure out the paper work and it's yours." He waited. "You've got what you wanted. Now what are you going to do?"

I didn't have a clue.

"Well, I did what you told me," Justin announced when he got home. "I did my job. I listened to the coach and he's moving me."

"Moving you?"

"Thanks to you and your great advice, he's taking me off defense and putting me up in mid. I'm no midfielder." He dropped onto the couch. "This is a disaster."

"I listened to my coach too, and I'm buying his coffee shop."

That got Justin's attention. "You're what? You can't run the business you got. What are you thinking, getting another one?"

"I'll sell the other one."

"Is it worth anything?"

"I guess I'll find out."

"You have to come back to practice on Saturday."

"Why's that?"

"Bad things happen to both of us when you don't."

17

THE PLAY ISN'T OVER IF THE BALL IS STILL IN BOUNDS

"I don't understand," Missy said as I walked into the office. "The Duncans are back. They said they made a mistake and they want to rebook us."

"I guess we better take care of them then."

I entered my office and didn't realize that she had meant they were literally back.

"Good morning," I said.

"Good morning. It would appear we were hasty in cancelling our plans with you."

"I'm glad we can work it out."

I wasn't really glad, but it was money. We got all the necessary paperwork in order and they left. Karen buzzed me from the front.

"You have a call on line two."

"Good morning," I said to the person on the other end of the line.

"I want to book a convention and I want you to handle it. I've heard good things about your firm. If you do it right, you stand to make a lot of money."

"I'm glad you've heard good things. It would be our pleasure to work with you. Can we sit down and discuss details?"

"I'm out of town, but I will email the complete package of information. If the work seems like something you can handle, just confirm by email and I'll send a bank draft to cover the deposit."

I was starting to get uncomfortable. This call was too easy. Work never came to us like this. I had to be sure.

"This sounds like a great contract. Who did you say referred you to us?"

"The Montague law firm that you did that outstanding fundraiser for last September to raise money for their client's daughter who had cancer."

I remembered that event. We had done a very good job. So, the call was legitimate. Maybe this was the answer to my prayers.

"Do you have my email address?"

"Yes. You can expect the package momentarily."

I hung up the phone and opened my email. I waited. What do they say about a watched pot? When the email arrived, it was better than I had hoped. He was right. The contract was substantial. It would really put us in a far better cash flow situation. We would have our work cut out for us, but we could do it.

I worked hard all day. It was the first time in a while that I completely lost track of time. So, when the phone rang and it was Justin wondering whether or not I was coming home for dinner, I was surprised.

"What time is it?" I asked.

"Almost 6:30."

"Wow. I didn't realize. Okay, I'll be home by 7:15. Can you start supper?"

"Sure. What is there?"

"I don't know, Justin. Open the fridge door. Open the freezer door. Open the cupboard door. I don't care. You're a big boy. Figure it out."

"Nice talking to you too, Mom." He hung up.

Perhaps I had been a little too abrupt. It wasn't his fault I had worked late without letting him know. And was this what happened to me when we got a little busy? I thought I should apologize when I got home.

Except when I got there, Justin wasn't. He left a note on the table. "Todd called. I went there for supper. His mother cooks." Two could play that game. I went back to work and when I got home around eleven, my note had been crumpled up and thrown on my bed, and Justin was asleep in his room.

I was late getting to Justin's game the next evening. He didn't even acknowledge me as he spotted me from across the field. I waved but there was no response. I settled in. They seemed to be doing better, although I wasn't exactly sure who they were playing.

The boys were running down the field. Justin kicked the ball to the forward. It looked like it was going to be out. The ball stopped short of the line.

"Get the ball," the coach screamed. "It's still in bounds. Play the ball."

The opposing team's defense got there first and the scoring opportunity was lost. If the boys hadn't given up. If they had played the chance they were given, they might have scored. We'd never know, because they didn't take the shot. They stopped short when they thought the ball was out of play. It reminded me a lot of my business. My ball was still in play it would appear. I had another shot to score. I wasn't going to waste this one. I had learned a lot about myself, my business, and myself in business. I was ready.

18

DEVELOP BOTH SIDES OF YOUR BODY

I was on fire. I was working both businesses and still managing to support Justin's soccer schedule. The events we planned were running smoothly and the referrals were generating more work. Drew was ecstatic. Karen was happy, although she was experiencing men troubles and so I couldn't really gauge her enthusiasm for the increased work. I was hoping that longer hours would restrict her contact with the type of people who were definitely bad choices for her, but I realized that I couldn't control her social life. Missy was a delight. She was working so hard. I could see potential in her.

"Thanks everybody," I said. "Things have gotten really busy around here and I see how hard you're working. I just want you to know I appreciate it."

They smiled. Well, the two girls did.

"Something bothering you, Drew?" I asked.

"I heard you're buying a coffee shop."

Busted.

"That's right."

"You didn't think we should know?"

"We got busy around the same time. I just didn't get the chance to talk to everyone."

"What are you going to do with this business?"

"Exactly what I am doing."

"You aren't going to sell it?"

"Do you want to buy it?" I challenged (in a nice way, of course.)

He shook his head and walked away.

"Drew, come back. I'm sorry. I have no plans to sell, but I will be looking to someone to take more responsibility and would consider developing a partnership for future consideration."

Drew came back. "So, you were serious about me buying it?"

"I wouldn't dismiss the thought."

"It's got to be more profitable than just one or two big gigs."

"So, help me get there." I glanced at Missy and Karen who had heard this whole conversation and had a look of panic. "It will take all of us. Are you in?"

The three of them nodded their heads. They were in.

I recognized that not telling them about the coffee shop was an error on my part. I didn't have to tell them how it happened or how miserable I had been, but I should have told them so they didn't hear it from someone else.

The truth was, it was exciting to know the business was improving and that I had options. I liked knowing that everything wasn't riding on one thing. It made it easier. I was actually much more creative. I had come up with some pretty unique concepts to pitch. We had run a couple of riverboat cruises for company executives and their families. We were negotiating a private concert using the local casino and their headliners. We had even quoted on providing a live theatre production in which an eccentric millionaire (who couldn't act) was going to play the lead and have the local newspaper provide glowing reviews. It was very time consuming, but well worth the effort when we saw signed contracts and cashed checks. I wasn't exactly sure what had turned things around, but I knew that the more I kept learning about myself, the better things seemed to be going at work.

It seemed I was doing what the coach had been working on with the boys. I was developing both sides of myself so I could double my play options. I had learned that lesson so well, that I could make plays with both sides of myself - creative and administrative; coffee shop and event planning, simultaneously. Oh yeah, I was writing the playbook on this one.

I have to admit that I wasn't seeing as much of Justin as I liked, but he was busy with soccer and summer stuff, so I wasn't too worried. He dropped by the office once in a while and seemed to be hanging around the reception desk talking to Missy. I could hear them talking and laughing. He was such a good kid.

"Hey, Mom, can I go with Missy to the bank?" he asked.

"Sure."

"Cool. We'll be back in a few."

I watched the two of them leave together. He held the door open for her and waved nonchalantly back at me. It suddenly occurred to me that perhaps my son was learning to develop both sides of another part of himself.

19

KNOW WHY YOU ARE PLAYING THE GAME

Life was crazy. The business had really taken off. I was working all kinds of hours, juggling the demands of planning, logistics, and overseeing the actual events. The busier we got, the less I focused on the big picture strategies that I knew were required to sustain what was happening to us. Nothing seemed broken, so nothing needed fixing – right?

Justin's soccer season was heading into the final stretch. He hadn't mentioned soccer camp and I didn't have time to pursue it with him. I knew that I really needed to understand how he had made the money to go so quickly, but for now, I was preoccupied with the money I was making.

"Here," he said as we walked back to the car following practice.

"What's this?" I asked.

"A letter to the parents, from the coach."

"What's it about?"

"Apparently, some of the parents don't like his style."

"Really?" I opened the letter. It was terse. 'Just a reminder, that I am the coach. I practice and play the boys as I see fit. If you don't like the way I coach, come talk to me. If your boy doesn't like me or the way I'm coaching, then maybe it's time to find another team. I don't have time or tolerance to babysit. We come to practice and win games. If you can't support me in that, then even at this point in the season, you better sign on with someone else.' I turned to Justin. "Why do you like to play soccer so much?"

"It's mine," he said without hesitation. "I can be as good or as lousy as I choose. The coach gives us drills and advice, but in the game, it's just us. We have to decide for ourselves. I like that. I don't really have that anywhere else in my life. I like to run. I like how it feels to stop someone from scoring. I just really love the game. It's all mine."

"Interesting."

"Why?"

"You spend a lot of time, developing your skill, getting yelled at, winning some, losing some. I was just curious."

Justin looked at me, considering, before he spoke again. "You're not around much, Mom. Is this what having a successful business means?"

I smiled. "I thought I was around too much."

"Just sometimes."

"Yeah, there's a certain amount of extra time I have to spend right now. But, you know, it's what we asked for – what you asked for."

"Me?"

"You said you didn't like being poor, so, working longer hours to make more money, is one way to stop being poor."

Justin shifted uncomfortably in his seat. "Soccer camp starts Monday."

"Already? Wow, where has the summer gone?"

"So, I can go?"

"You told me you were registered and that you had the money, so I guess you're going."

"But you didn't believe me, about the money."

"You said you earned it."

"Okay." Justin relaxed. "Cool. Mom?"

"Yes."

"Why are you playing?"

"Playing what?"

"Well, I guess you're not playing, exactly, but why are you in business? Remember I asked you that a few weeks ago and you didn't really have an answer?" I nodded. "I just wondered if you knew now?"

"It pays the bills."

"That's still not a great answer."

I knew that. It was interesting to have to think about that question again. Before, I blamed the fact that the business wasn't doing well, as the reason that I didn't enjoy 'playing', but the fact was, that the business was doing very well, and I didn't enjoy it any more than before. I was still playing for the wrong reasons, but anyone in their right mind would question me getting out now.

"I have to get back," I called out to Justin as he unlocked the back door. It was the story of my life lately, running out for reasons only thinly disguised as important.

I still stopped by the coffee shop to get my caffeine and coaching fix. Peter had a way of setting me back upright and sending me off to conquer the world.

"Should I need a jolt of java and you to get me going?" I asked.

"No," he replied simply. "And you only ever need it when you have to go to your other office."

"True," I admitted more to myself than to him. "Why is that?"

"You already know the answer to that."

He was right. It wasn't about the money the business was making. It wasn't about the powerful people who were now calling us and dropping by. It wasn't about the lavish events we could create. It was far more basic. It was about the quality of the relationships. That was the problem everywhere. Money didn't replace people. Success didn't equal fulfillment. Even when I was getting it right, I was getting it wrong.

I decided right there to sell the event business. I would ask Drew and Karen if they wanted to buy it. I would find someone and I wouldn't get in such a hurry to unload it that I took a financial soaking either. I was going to apply everything I had learned to make a smart business decision for a change.

There were just a few loose details for large contracts to take care of first.

20

Review the previous game's outcome before the next game

"Practice might run a little long tonight," Justin informed me as we pulled into the parking lot.

"How come?"

"Coach wants to go over our last game before Thursday."

"Okay."

"Are you staying?"

I could tell by the look on his face that he wanted me to. "For a few minutes."

The boys gathered on the field in a circle around the coach.

"Last week's game sucked," he began.

"But coach, we won."

"You didn't deserve to win. You didn't even try. When you are outplayed, I get that, but this wasn't about skill. Did you think you were too good to put in a little effort because you were playing against a poorer team? It was pathetic. Most of you might as well have stayed home or sent your mothers to play for you." Justin turned to look at me and grinned. "It's important to review the previous game to see where you can improve before you take to the field the next time, but I got nothing to say about that. How can I tell you where to improve when I didn't see anything at all to even comment on?"

I thought about that as I reflected on the eventual sale of one business and my transition to another one. What had I learned? What game review did I need to have before taking on another 'team'? I decided to have a little pep talk of my own. With myself. So, I went back to the car, once the coach starting with a few running drills.

"Play Review," I spoke aloud. "What I learned about myself, about business, and about myself in business.

1. I like owning a business better than working for someone else.

2. I enjoy being around people.

3. I enjoy talking and laughing.

4. I make people feel good when they talk to me.

5. I need to feel fulfilled in my work.

6. A business should be based on passion, not necessity, if I want to be able to carry it through good times and bad.

7. A business is a business when it provides a service that people are willing to pay for and there are systems in place to track what's going on.

8. There are parts of running my current business that I don't like and that I don't do well.

9. I know what those parts are and I have a plan to compensate for that in the next business (okay that one wasn't exactly true, yet, but I was working on it).

10. Successful businesses have a plan and an owner that can work the plan.

11. You can't force yourself to be a type of business owner that you aren't.

12. I can only develop a business as much as I am willing to develop myself.

13. I have to know why I'm playing the game.

14. I have to leave it all on the field.

15. I have to review the previous game and learn everything there is to learn from that experience, before I suit up again.

What a great little business handbook I had developed. I didn't realize that I spent the entire practice jotting down my thoughts, so when Justin tapped on the window, I nearly leapt through the roof.

"What is wrong with you?" I barked through the glass.

"Chill. Practice is done, but coach wants to take us for an iced capp. Can I go?"

I was still startled by the window thing. "Do you mean I sat here for two hours, only now to be told it will be another 45 minutes before we can go home?" I sounded more agitated than I was, but it was too late.

"Fine," he hissed. "I'll tell him I can't go."

"I didn't say that."

"No, it's fine. I don't want to go anyway."

And they say teen girls are moody!

"Go ahead. I don't want you to miss out if it's some team bonding thing." That didn't come out quite right, either.

"Nice, Mom. That's much better." He walked to his side, opened the door, dropped onto the seat, and slammed the door shut. "Let's go."

"I'm sorry. I didn't mean for it to sound like it did."

"Let's just go."

"Shouldn't you tell the coach?"

"I said let's go."

Needless to say, it was a quiet ride home. I wasn't sure whether talking or continued silence was the answer, so I opted for the latter, knowing that once I did engage in conversation, I had no idea what I wanted to say anyway.

21

IF YOU'RE GOING TO PLAY, SOMETIMES YOU GET HIT

Life was good. *Better Events* was thriving and the business valuation was complete. Drew and Karen had drafted a partnership agreement. We were negotiating terms for them to take over in 60 days. I felt happier and freer than I ever had. I was looking longingly at the slower pace of the coffee shop. I was running from location to location, trying to tie up loose ends and keep it together. I wasn't home much, but I had told Justin that the light was definitely at the end of the tunnel.

"How's camp?" I asked as we grabbed breakfast in motion.

"Pretty good."

"What kinds of things are you learning?"

He stared at me. "You don't have to try so hard. I know you're busy with your stuff."

"Justin," I didn't get a chance to finish.

"Forget it, Mom. I'll tell you when you're really listening and not just checking the box."

"I wasn't."

"Yeah, you were. You've been doing it for a while." He grabbed his bag. "I've got a ride with Chris's dad this morning, so you don't have to drive me." And then he was gone.

I didn't really understand what had just happened or how we had grown apart so quickly. It was confusing, trying to raise a son on my own. I didn't understand his moods any better than I did my own sometimes. But I knew that I loved him. I knew that I was making the choices I was because I loved him. I knew that counted for something. It had to.

I cleaned up the kitchen and quickly dressed. This was a big day. I was meeting Drew and Karen at the lawyer's, then taking my check to deposit at the bank. Today was THE day. It was all coming together, just as I had planned.

I dropped by the coffee shop to fill Peter in on the latest details of the deal. We had visited for a few minutes when he abruptly changed the topic.

"How's Justin with all this?"

"You know. He's a kid."

"Don't let him hear you say that."

"I just don't understand. I thought he got it. He knows I have to do what I'm doing to be able to get out of *Better Events*, but he's so mad at me all the time."

"Maybe your worlds are clashing right now."

"Maybe." I looked at my watch. "I have to go. I better call Drew and let him know I'm on my way." I dug around in my purse and realized that I had left my cell phone on the kitchen counter. "Can I use your phone?"

I got to the lawyer's office with about two minutes to spare. Thankfully, she was running a bit behind so no harm done. Drew and Karen were talking excitedly between themselves. I was almost envious. They would do a great job running the business together. I wished that I had had someone to talk things over with, be creative with, worry with, but that wasn't how it had been. It might have been a different business for me if I had had that, but there wasn't any point in rewriting history.

The meeting ran a little longer than I had expected, but it was done. *Better Events* was officially sold. I held the check tentatively in my hand. There it was, a single piece of paper representing the financial value of my work. It was interesting how anticlimactic it was. I had put a great deal of energy, resources, and time into the business, and yet to be finished with it didn't really give me the feelings of liberation that I had anticipated.

As I was walking out of the office, I heard Drew call out to me.

"Liz. Liz, wait."

Oh no, I thought. He has changed his mind. Walk faster. Run if you have to, just get the check to the bank before he catches you.

"Liz, it's Justin."

I froze. Justin? Why would he be calling Drew?

"Liz, it's the hospital. You better take the call."

What met me at the hospital was even more traumatizing than the call that Justin had been injured at the soccer camp and was taken by ambulance to emergency. There, standing near the nurse's desk, looking very concerned and quite parental, was my ex-husband.

"About time you got here," he snapped.

I felt all the old insecurities well up inside. I was a horrible mother. I had abandoned my son in his hour of greatest need. And worst of all, I had created a situation where Justin's father would be the hero.

"I came as soon as I got the call," I felt myself stumbling over the words that had been so hard to retrieve from my throat.

"Well, that's the problem. No one was able to get you."

I walked past him, to the desk. "I'm Justin Robertson's mother. May I see my son?"

I was led to examination room 3. Justin looked so fragile lying in the bed. His eyes were closed. I gently touched his hand.

"Where were you?"

"At the lawyer's."

"I couldn't get you."

"I know. I'm sorry. I forgot my phone this morning."

"I needed you, Mom."

"I'm sorry."

"They called Dad."

"I know."

"Is he still here?"

"Yes."

"I didn't want them to call him, Mom, but they had to."

"I know. Well, the good news is that his phone is hooked up again." I couldn't get over how lame I sounded. I sure knew a lot when it was too late. "What happened?"

"I got knocked out. The doctor said I have a concussion and my nose might be broken."

"I'm sorry."

"Dad came right away."

"That's good."

"No, it isn't. I don't want to owe him."

"You don't."

"Yes, I will. That's how it works."

"No, Justin."

"You don't know, Mom. You don't know anything." He turned away from me. I thought I saw a tear roll down his cheek, but I said nothing.

"You're going to be okay, honey."

"Don't call me that. I'm not a baby anymore, Mom."

"Sorry."

"For what? For choosing your business over me? For not being there when I needed you? Or for marrying a jerk like Dad in the first place?"

"I understand you're upset with me, Justin," I began.

"I'm way past upset, Mom."

Jim appeared at the door, suddenly. His timing was always impeccable. "I talked to the doctor. Your nose is broken." Neither of us spoke. "What's going on?"

"Thanks for coming." Justin spoke.

"No problem. That's what a Dad's for, right?"

"Sure." There was an oppressive silence in the room. "You can go, now," Justin suggested.

"I can stay for a while."

"Maybe he doesn't want you to," I offered.

"I think he's old enough to speak for himself, don't you?"

"I did. I want you to go."

"That's pretty selfish, don't you think? I came all the way down here."

"I already said thank you."

"Whatever." He turned to leave.

"No. Wait." I wondered why Justin would stop his father when he was so close to going.

"I wish you hadn't come, at all. Then I would have known you were a lousy person. Now, I know you're just a lousy dad."

"Don't you talk to me like that," Jim snarled. Justin rolled over. "Look at me!" He grabbed Justin's shoulder, attempting to flip him back, but not realizing his son had become a young man. With one fluid move, Justin grabbed his dad's arm and freed himself.

"Don't you EVER touch me again," he told Jim.

And just as quickly as he had come, Jim was gone. I couldn't speak.

"Are you leaving, too?" Justin asked. I shook my head. "Don't you have to go somewhere?"

"No," I whispered.

"No business to take care of?"

"No."

"Amazing how important I am to everybody when I'm hurt."

"Justin, that's not fair."

"Not fair? You want to talk to me about not fair? I've been in second place to everything else. I can't even get your attention lately unless I'm mad at you."

"I know. I've been distracted. But things are going to get better. You'll see."

"Because you've switched disasters? I don't get it. Why another business? When will you realize that you're no good at it?"

"I think I am. I just had to find the right business."

"Wow. So, I have to suffer while you figure it out? I'm tired of our life, Mom. I don't want to be the poorest kid in my class any more. I don't want to be embarrassed because my stuff is held together by pins and tape. I don't want to have to steal money from you to pay for soccer camp." He stopped suddenly. What had he just said?

"Steal money from me?"

He started to sob.

"But you said you had a job."

"I never found one. I didn't want you to be disappointed again."

"So, you lied to me?"

"I'm sorry."

"But I never have that kind of cash in my wallet."

"I didn't take it from your purse."

"Then how?"

"That time I went to the bank with Missy."

I was horrified. "You took it from the bank deposit?"

He didn't have to answer. I could tell.

"I thought Missy had taken the money. I accused her of being irresponsible and a thief. I fired her, Justin."

"I'm sorry, Mom."

It hardly mattered in that moment. I felt like someone had just punched me in the stomach. And the head. And the heart.

22

YOU SPEND TIME ON WHAT YOU VALUE

The next few days were an absolute blur. My mind couldn't wrap itself around the fact that Justin had felt that his only solution was to take the money. I was so angry, and hurt, and disappointed. I also blamed myself. If I had been more responsive. If I had been more attentive. If I had been a better business owner, better mother, better human being. I would have probably accepted responsibility for global warming and world hunger, if someone had accused me. Justin used to tease me that that was one of my favorite sayings, but he wasn't doing much teasing these days and I probably wouldn't have been very receptive to him anyway. Once I explained to Drew and Karen what had happened to Justin at soccer, there was no problem in shortening the business transition time for sixty days to twelve hours. I called Peter and told him I needed a few extra days to close the deal on the coffee shop and he was very accommodating as well. It was reassuring that not everyone in my world had become someone I didn't recognize.

I tapped lightly on Justin's door, "Can I come in?"

"Sure."

"How are you feeling today?"

"Okay. Did the doctor say I could go back to soccer?"

"You can start practicing with the team again next week - just simple drills, no contact yet."

"Next week? But we play Jenson's on Thursday."

"Give yourself some time to heal."

I sat down on the bed beside him. "Justin, we have to talk about it."

"It wasn't my fault. The guy hit me from behind."

"Not how you got hurt. I already talked to the coach about that. I mean the," I hesitated, not sure how to say it, "the money."

Justin looked away. "I'm really sorry I told you about that."

"I fired a perfectly innocent young woman. How do you suppose that makes me look?"

"So, now this is about you?"

"Justin, it IS about me, but not in the way you think. My own son felt he had no choices but to steal money from my business. How is that not about me?" I paused for effect. "Why didn't you talk to me?"

Justin looked confused. "I did talk to you. You weren't listening. Soccer is the only thing I care about. I want to be good, Mom. You should appreciate that. Don't you want to be good at business? Isn't that why you were willing to do anything to hang on to it?" He had a point. "I had to go, Mom. All the guys on my team were going to camp. Coach said we had to go. But you didn't care."

I put my hand in the air to stop him. I could feel the lump welling in my throat. "Justin. It isn't that I didn't care. It has never been that."

"It sure felt like it. Nothing seemed to be as important as the business. You were always there. And you taught me that people spend time on what they value. I played soccer. You worked. So, I assumed that's what mattered most to you."

"I'm here now."

"Because you have to be."

"That's not true. I want to be. I do value you and our relationship. It's why I sold Better Events. It's why I bought the coffee shop. For us. So we can have a better life."

"Then why not ask me what I want?"

"What?"

"How do you know what a better life means for me if you've never asked?"

"And if I had asked, what would you have said?"

"Show me the money!"

I smiled. He did have a way of making things simple.

"Do you think money is the only answer to a better life?"

"From where I stand."

I smiled again. "I'm sure." I took a couple of moments to consider my next words carefully. "I've had money. Lots of it. Before I married your dad. It was his carefree attitude that attracted me to him in the first place. He wasn't about material possessions." I stopped to reflect. "Let me rephrase. He didn't want to acquire material possessions, just waste mine. We went through a great deal of cash in a short period of time. I saw firsthand that having money is not the answer. In fact, it put a wedge between us that eventually broke us up. We were philosophically so different on so many fronts, we just couldn't make it work."

"You were loaded?"

I wished he could get past that and see the point I was trying to make, but he was, after all, only fourteen.

"Yes."

"So, how could you let this happen?" I look at him, puzzled. "How could you get so poor and let me suffer? You hooked Dad up, but you hung me out."

"Not on purpose. I don't really like having no money, either, in case you didn't know. I wanted you to learn that working hard for what you get is important. To follow your dreams. To make it happen on your own."

"I would have read the book. I didn't need to take the course."

"Funny. But at some point, I realized that it didn't have to be hard work. That I had jumped into something without really knowing what my dream was. I had missed something pretty important, so when you suggested I get a mentor, I sought out someone who looked like they had done what I hadn't."

"Peter?"

"Yes. He asked me some challenging questions about myself and about business. I didn't like it, but he held up the mirror. I realized that what I saw was what I was getting."

"What was that, Mom?"

"Less than I wanted."

"And what is the coffee shop going to do for you?"

"It is the dream. I love people. I love small intimate spaces where people gather and share their lives. I want to create a community for us, Justin. I want you to work there with me. I've been wondering how I can punish you for taking the money, but realized that it isn't about that. Sure, you have to know that what you did was wrong, but I think you already know that. You have to pay the money back. But I want you to learn more than that, otherwise we're right back to money being the most important thing. For me, it's about the relationship. I failed you somehow in our relationship, that you believed it was okay to steal from me. I can't undo that, but I can change, go forward, so you will never be okay with that type of choice again."

Justin hung his head. "I am sorry, Mom. For everything."

"Me, too. But we have choices. We have to move on. I've called Missy's parents to apologize and I offered Missy a part time job at the coffee shop. It will be up to you to make things right with her."

"Will you ever trust me again?"

"I hope so. That's up to you. I'm giving you the chance. You will be in the coffee shop with me, hand in the cash register. It will be up to you what you do."

"You're a good mom."

"It is my first priority. It always has been."

I put my arm around him. "Are you too old for a hug?"

He smiled, "I used to be."

23

WIN EACH HALF ON ITS OWN

The doctor let Justin return to the team for the last two games before playoffs. He was ready. In fact, his first game back was probably the best of his season. His feet were on fire, and his shots true. He stopped the superstar from the other team and completely frustrated the offensive line. I smiled more broadly and cheered more loudly as the game developed. But no one player can make the game, so at the end of the first half they were down by two.

The boys jogged on the field for the second half as though they had just arrived. They ignited their game and by the final whistle had rallied to a three – two victory. They engaged in their customary ceremonial dance and then headed to the bench for words from the coach. I lingered on the sidelines, packing up my chair, and remembering how cold and wet we had all started out this season. But today, the sun was shining and the warmth reassured me that conditions change continuously and what was a setback yesterday, can be a setup for today.

I watched Justin walk across the pitch. He loved this game. He was laughing and goofing around with his teammates. The coach gave him a slap on the back. It was all good.

"Great game," I told him.

"Not bad." He grinned. "It felt sooooo good to be back."

"I could tell. You looked good out there."

"It took a few minutes to get my game on."

"Not just you. What did the coach say at half time? It was a different team that took the field."

"He just reminded us of what he had said at practice."

"Which was?" I prompted.

"Play each half on its own."

"What does that mean?"

"Well. The first half was gone. We couldn't change the score. But if we focused on that then we would play the second half as losers. We aren't losers, Mom, so we played the second half as though we were starting over."

"Brilliant."

"Kind of like us." He gave me a gentle push.

"Is that what we're doing?"

"Yeah. We're playing our second half."

I liked that.

"The coach wants to take everyone out for ice cream. Can I go?"

"Certainly."

He started back across the field, then stopped. "You want to come?"

"Sure, but I'll sit with the other parents, okay?"

"You don't have to. But thanks."

He had come a long way. He wasn't the same kid since I had sold Better Events and started running the coffee shop. He always came right after school and spent at least an hour with me, depending on his homework. He had even come up with special promotions to encourage the other kids from his school to drop by once in a while. I don't mean that we didn't still have parent-child issues. I would have been more concerned if we didn't, but it was the normal stuff that one can expect when children mature and test the boundaries.

"You're a good mom."

"So you've said." He turned away. "And Justin?"

"Yeah."

"You're a good son."

He grinned and I winked.

I drove by the coffee shop slowly on the way home. It was ours. A business built on dreams and hard work, nestled in love, and thriving on personal values. I looked over at Justin who was riding along, eyes closed, replaying the game in his head.

I had it all.

Epilogue

Stay in the game until the final whistle

The years passed too quickly. I blinked and Justin was grown. He had received a scholarship to play soccer for a great school and had then been drafted his first year to play professionally. My son was playing professional ball. Once in a while he would drop by the coffee shop and sign autographs and pour coffee. I had asked him if he wasn't too famous to be serving patrons at his mother's coffee shop and he told me that he would never have gotten where he was if it hadn't been for his mother and her coffee shop and that he would never think of himself as too good to be of service to others.

The Better Brew, as it was now known, had given us a good life. A better life. We had always had enough money to meet our needs and enough work to build our characters. We had learned about life and business while growing our relationships.

I had applied perhaps the most important lesson that I had learned that summer long ago from Justin's coach: stay in the game until the final whistle. My final whistle hadn't yet blown and so I was in it, giving all that I had so when Justin called late at night after a game, we could let each other know that we had left it all on the field. His on the soccer pitch. And mine on the business pitch.

QUESTIONS TO CONSIDER WHEN APPLYING THE THEMES OF THE PITCH TO YOUR LIFE AND BUSINESS:

- If inadequately prepared, how can you expect your business to do any better?

- Goal realization is all about the right combination of the love of the game and high performance expectations. How successfully are you reaching your goals?

- Have you really done all that is necessary to understand the game and the rules of engagement?

- How current is your business plan? Did you have one at all?

- What impression would a potential client get about your business upon entering your work environment?

- Write down everything it takes to run your business. Who is or will be doing each of those things?

- Why are you even in this game?

- If your business is to grow, you have to nurture the people who can help you. How are you nurturing your current relationships?

Linda J. Lord is an author, producer, and performer. She blends real life with creativity to provide options for people looking for better ways to work and live. Linda formed Creative Class Productions to provide a home for creativity, business, and life.

Linda lives in Canada with her husband, children, two cats, and one dog.